The Lost Sheep

The Lost Sheep

My Unlikely Odyssey With Billy Blankenship

a novel by

Jeff Call

Provo, Utah

This is a work of fiction. The characters, names, incidents, places, and dialogue are products of the author's imagination, and are not to be construed as real.

ISBN 13: 978-1-932898-80-4
e. 1

Published by:
Spring Creek Book Company
P.O. Box 50355
Provo, Utah 84605-0355

www.springcreekbooks.com

Printed in the United States of America
10 9 8 7 6 5 4 3 2 1
Printed on acid-free paper

Library of Congress Cataloging-in-Publication Data

Call, Jeff, 1968-
The lost sheep : my unlikely odyssey with Billy Blankenship / by Jeff Call.
p. cm.
ISBN 978-1-932898-80-4 (pbk. : alk. paper)
1. Mormons--Fiction. I. Title.

PS3603.A44L67 2007
813'.6--dc22

2007023697

Dedication

To my wife CherRon and my sons Ryan, Brayden, Landon, Austin, Carson, and Janson.

CHAPTER 1

The Primary Cause of Our Primary Problems

During my years in Primary, I learned that Jesus Christ loves everyone, especially children. I learned about Jesus Christ taking upon himself all of the sins of every person who ever lived, and who would ever live, in this world.

You know what the most amazing thing was? That the Savior could love someone like Billy Blankenship.

Billy was one of those kids people never forgot, no matter how hard they tried.

My name is Kevin Russell, and it's been almost 30 years since Billy and I attended Primary together—we were the same age—and I can still see his wiry frame coiled on a metal chair, whirling around during the opening song like a Tasmanian Devil hopped up on sugar, firing a rubber band at some poor kid's head, then cackling like the Wicked Witch of the West.

He was loud, crude and belligerent, and those were some of his better qualities. He sported a horror-movie grin, perpetually dirty fingernails, and charcoal-black hair that looked like it had been combed with a firecracker.

Billy was the most bizarre circus act this side of Barnum & Bailey. He showed off his double-jointed arms and he made his bones snap, crackle and pop in grotesque fashion. Like fingernails on a chalkboard, he grated on everybody around him.

He wore grungy shoes, pants that were three sizes too small, and wrinkled shirts soiled with ketchup stains. At least, I think it was ketchup. Knowing Billy, it might have been blood. He regaled us with stories of the crazy things he enjoyed doing, like getting on his skateboard to take rides on the back bumpers of moving cars, shimmying up 20-foot-tall flag poles, and jumping off the roof of his house, which explained the assorted bumps, bruises and abrasions on his body. Billy must have broken his arm three times in elementary school, and he was proud of it. He bragged that he was going to be a Hollywood stuntman someday.

Speaking of Hollywood, Billy was a television addict. Without provocation, he randomly and frequently quoted lines from TV shows or TV commercials. For example, he claimed he was "bionic," like *The Six Million Dollar Man*. Sometimes he'd move in slow motion and imitate the accompanying electronic sound effects like the show, which got annoying.

From time to time, he'd parrot that line from *The Incredible Hulk*, "Don't make me angry. You wouldn't like me when I'm angry!" That, I knew, was true. Nobody liked him when he was angry—or when he was in any other mood.

While most of us kids were reading *Charlie and the Chocolate Factory*, Billy was watching *Charlie's Angels* on TV. Some people blamed television for inculcating him with such warped, deranged behavior.

When an abandoned house in our neighborhood went up in flames one summer, Billy was the prime suspect. He was always playing around that run-down shack and a couple of kids said they saw him there goofing around with a cigarette lighter. It was a three-alarm blaze, sending fire trucks racing into our quiet neighborhood. Luckily, no other homes were threatened by the flames. Everyone suspected Billy had started the fire, and some of the adults accused him of arson, but nobody could prove it.

That day, a fireman lectured us neighborhood kids about not playing with matches. "You know what they call it when someone intentionally starts fires?" he asked us. "Arson. And if you commit arson, you can go to prison for a very long time."

"What do you call a person who starts fires?" Billy asked.

"An arsonist," the fireman said. Billy smiled proudly, as if he had just added another title to his résumé.

Yes, Billy Blankenship was The Boy Nobody Wanted Their Daughters to Marry and he would have been voted Most Likely to End Up In the State Penitentiary.

The way most people in our southern California ward saw it, Billy put the "suffer" in "suffer the little children to come unto me." A few people said the only good thing about Billy was that he was an only child. Terrified kids referred to him as "Bully" Blankenship. Exasperated adults referred to him as "Billy blankety-blank Blankenship."

These days, Billy probably would have been diagnosed with some psychological disorder, prescribed a pharmacy full of medications, and remanded to a troubled youth facility. Chances are that he would have undergone years of counseling and we probably never would have had to deal with him.

But back then we weren't that lucky.

Billy was nine when he moved into our ward, and he wasted little time establishing his reputation. On his first day in Primary, Sister Leftwich made the mistake of telling him, "Since you aren't going to pay attention to this lesson that I spent hours preparing this week, then why don't you come up here and teach the class yourself."

Without pausing, Billy bounced off his seat, stood in front of the class and started a belching contest. That was the last time we saw Sister Leftwich. She put her house up for sale before the following week.

During our years in Primary together, we had a revolving door of teachers because Billy had driven a countless number of them away. Teaching our class wasn't a calling, it was torture.

With Billy, Primary teachers couldn't use the standby threat,

"If you don't fold your arms and listen, I'll get your dad to sit in here with you."

That's because Billy's dad didn't go to church. Billy's mom attended church faithfully every week, but I guess nobody ever asked her to discipline him because they figured she had enough of him the other six days of the week. Everyone felt sorry for her, but nobody knew how to help. Billy's mother dragged him to church meetings, probably in hopes that it would reform him somehow by osmosis. But every year he moved on to the new class without really learning anything about the gospel. It's not like you can get "held back" in Primary.

Billy never sang Primary songs, at least not the right way. He liked to make up his own lyrics. "Give Said the Little Stream" became "You Better Give Me An Ice Cream" and "I Hope They Call Me On A Mission" became "After Church I'm Going to Go Fishin'."

At church, he would entertain himself by asking his mom to read the name of a hymn out of the hymnbook. He'd repeat the title and add "in the bathroom" to the end of it. So "The Time Is Far Spent" became "The Time Is Far Spent *in the Bathroom*."

"I Stand All Amazed" became "I Stand All Amazed *in the Bathroom*."

"Now Let Us Rejoice" became "Now Let Us Rejoice *in the Bathroom*."

You get the idea.

He'd say each one aloud and howl with laughter. I have to admit, I thought some of them were pretty funny, though I tried hard not to laugh. When I started to snicker, my mom would flash me one of those you're-in-trouble-when-we-get-home looks.

My mom, bless her heart, was the Primary President for those years that Billy was in Primary. She held weekly presidency meetings at our house and Billy was always one of the prime topics of discussion. Because of Billy Blankenship, the noise level in Primary was comparable to the runway at the Los Angeles International Airport.

Stories about Billy spread like wildfire throughout the wards and stakes of southern California. I guess you could say he became a notorious legend, a Mormon version of Billy the Kid. It got to the point that the stake sent a spy to find out how terrible Billy really was. A dour, gray-haired high councilman, carrying a briefcase, wandered inside our classroom.

"Who's the old guy?" Billy asked as the high councilman sat down.

After observing Billy telling off-color jokes, burping, and sticking his head out the window, the high councilman walked over to Billy's seat and glowered at him through bifocals.

"Young man, your behavior is appalling," he said, sticking his wrinkled, crooked finger in Billy's chest.

"Thanks," Billy said.

"That's not a compliment, young man," the high councilman replied. "I want you to stand against the wall for rest of the class."

"Fine," Billy said. "I'd rather stand here than sit in those stupid hard chairs anyway."

Then the elderly man began to preach us a sermon, teaching us about repentance, and how every time we sin—like being irreverent in class—it's like carrying a heavy burden.

"Pick up my briefcase," he said to Billy, who left his spot against the wall and, uncharacteristically, did as he was told.

"It's heavy, isn't it?" the high councilman asked.

"No," Billy snapped. "It's not heavy at all. Watch!"

Billy raced out the door, briefcase in hand. The high councilman gave chase, shuffling after Billy. Moments later, we looked out the classroom window and saw Billy darting around the parking lot, with the high councilman following as if in slow motion. Billy taunted the old man by allowing him to get within arm's reach and sticking the briefcase in front of him, then quickly pulling it away while laughing demonically.

All of us kids started laughing at the sight, too, until the old man stopped, clutched his chest and dropped to the ground like a sack of dried prunes. Someone called the paramedics, who said the high councilman had suffered a heart attack. The old man lived, but I was sure that Billy wouldn't live to see age 12.

Billy never listened to the teachers or other leaders; he never learned anything in Primary about being reverent or being kind to others. One time a boy named Stephen, who was just visiting, came to our Primary class. The teacher did what he could to make him feel welcome and comfortable, but Billy sat through the entire class making disgusting faces at the kid and kicking him in the shins. Then when class let out and we were walking down the hallway to find our parents, Billy stuffed a crumpled-up piece of paper down the back of his shirt and ran away. I remember Stephen standing alone in the hallway, crying. My mom asked me about it later. I just shrugged my shoulders.

"Kevin Theodore Russell, when something like that happens, you need to let me know," she scolded.

I wasn't sure about that. First of all, it wasn't cool to tattle. Second of all, I was scared to death of Billy. Most kids were. If you looked at Billy the wrong way, he'd threaten to go home and bring back his numchucks and beat you with them. Plus, he told everyone that he knew Kung Fu and when he got mad, he'd show off some of his moves. His eyes would go as big as frisbees and he'd start wildly swinging his arms and kicking his legs, screaming in some bizarre language.

A teacher at school once asked him to clean up his desk and he responded by dumping pencils and rulers onto the floor and throwing his books against the wall. That earned him a week of detention. Of course, Billy spent more time in detention than he did in class.

Sometimes, when my parents thought I was asleep, I overheard them talking about Billy and all of the troubles he caused the Primary. My mom tried her best to love Billy, I think, but it was hard for her, or anyone, to like him—let alone love him.

During those years, Billy and I were in the same school classes, too, but we definitely were not friends. That all changed when I was eleven years old, and Sister Browning became our Primary teacher.

CHAPTER 2

The Unsinkable Sister Browning

There was plenty to look forward to the year I turned 12 and near the top of my list was graduating from Primary.

I was excited to leave Primary because I felt like I had outgrown it like a pair of old shoes. The Primary chorister always talked to us like we were five-year-olds. I wanted to move on to bigger and better things.

I couldn't wait to turn 12 because I would receive the Aaronic Priesthood and become a Boy Scout. It was a rite of passage into manhood I couldn't wait to experience for myself. I had watched my older brothers go through it and I wanted to, too. But first, I had to endure my final year of Primary.

A couple of days after Christmas, as we were taking down our stockings, my mom broke the news to me. "Kevin, you're getting a new Primary teacher this week," she said enthusiastically.

My mom had uttered that phrase many times before, so I was significantly less enthusiastic about it than she was. "Who is Billy's next victim?" I asked, rolling my eyes.

"Her name is Sister Browning."

"Never heard of her."

She explained that Sister Browning was a young, single woman who had just moved into the ward. Sister Browning had served a mission to Italy, recently graduated from Brigham Young University and came to southern California to teach at the local high school. I didn't think much about it.

A couple of days later, Sister Browning stopped by our house to pick up the Primary manual. I have to admit, I liked her right away. She had long, curly brown hair that cascaded around her shoulders and framed her soft blue eyes. She was younger, and prettier, than the other teachers we had. Not only that, but she was very nice.

"It's great to meet you, Kevin," she said, placing her arm on my shoulders. "I can't wait to teach your class." None of our teachers had ever told us that before.

Mom warned Sister Browning about Billy and related the stories about him shooting out the neighbor's porch light with a BB gun; letting loose a jar full of spiders at the school; and ruining Gabriela Rodriguez's new dress by sticking a giant wad of gum on her chair. All in the same week.

I cringed as my mom told Sister Browning those things about Billy, hoping it didn't scare her off. But she seemed undaunted. "I like challenges," Sister Browning said, then winked at me. I blushed.

I'm sure I wasn't the first kid to have a secret crush on his Primary teacher. After she left, I scampered to the living room window and watched her walk to her car and drive away in her light green Volkswagen Bug.

I kind of felt bad for Sister Browning. Billy, I figured, would chew this woman up and spit her out like a handful of sunflower seeds, just as he had done to all of our other teachers.

When we were ten, Bishop Sweeten called Brother Murdock to teach our class. Brother Murdock was a built like an armored tank and rumor was that he had been a Marine drill sergeant. I think Bishop Sweeten figured that he could intimidate, or maybe even coerce, Billy into sitting quietly and paying attention.

While Brother Murdock turned his back to write something on the chalkboard, Billy threw a spit wad at the wall. While Brother Murdock looked down to read a scripture, Billy turned off the lights. While Brother Murdock shared a poignant personal experience, Billy moaned, "Booooorrrrring!"

Well, you could practically see the steam rising out of Brother Murdock's ears. As he tried reading another scripture, Billy interrupted by reciting poetry in his patented, shrill voice.

Spring has sprung, flowers have risen,
Here we sit in this crummy church prison!

The next time Brother Murdock turned his back, Billy slugged Chandler McCaffery in the stomach for no apparent reason. The blow was so forceful that Chandler turned blue and stopped breathing for several seconds.

Brother Murdock grabbed Billy by the shirt collar, shoved him outside the classroom door and told him not to come back.

Billy walked down the hall and pulled the fire alarm, clearing out the building in five minutes. Everyone suspected that Billy had done it, but nobody actually saw him. After that, Bishop Sweeten implemented what was known among the Primary teachers as the "Billy Blankenship Rule," which meant no child could be expelled from class unless accompanied by a member of the bishopric or one of the child's parents.

Brother Flynn was called to be our teacher around the Fourth of July. That week, Billy pulled a firecracker out of his pocket, lit it with a cigarette lighter and threw it on the floor.

BOOM!

The kids screamed and scattered. The noise startled Brother Flynn so badly that he jumped about three feet off the ground. He injured his back and ended up in traction for three weeks.

Sister Hart heard Billy swear in class and asked Bishop Sweeten to expel him permanently from Primary. That's exactly what Billy wanted. But Bishop Sweeten said no, much to the dismay of both Billy and the teacher. "We don't ever turn anyone away from Primary," he said. "Ever. The Lord loves all children."

When the bishop asked Brother Connelly to teach our class, he flatly turned him down. "I don't think my insurance covers that," he said. By trade, Brother Connelly was an undercover policeman.

Sister Westover had us vote on a class president that could sit wherever he or she wanted and could choose someone for the closing prayer (Billy refused to pray, so nobody ever called on him). We came up with class rules, like no spitting or swearing or name-calling. Of course, all of the rules were custom-made for Billy. He was the one who needed the rules. Trouble was, he didn't believe in rules, and he defied them just to prove that point.

Anyway, Sister Browning seemed real nice and I was sure she didn't know what she was getting herself into.

The first week of the New Year, she introduced herself to our class. She was so perky and happy, I wondered if she were real or if she just walked off the cover of a Church magazine. I figured that it was because she hadn't met Billy yet.

"I give her two weeks, tops," one of my friends, Todd Blackhurst, whispered to me.

Primary began in typical fashion with Billy knocking Skyler Cherrington's glasses to the floor.

Though he was only 11, Skyler must have weighed nearly 200 pounds. He sported three chins and one heck of a superiority complex. His reddish-orange hair complemented his mayonnaise-white skin, which was bespattered with freckles ("Those aren't freckles, sweetheart," his mother would tell him, "they're sun kisses."). He wore large glasses, which he called "spectacles." The lenses were about the size of hula hoops and they rested on his chubby cheeks.

He started wearing glasses at the age of six, announcing to our class at the time that he was far-sighted and with his new spectacles he had "20-15 vision" and could see "as well as a red-tailed hawk." Without his glasses, Skyler was blinder than a one-eyed rhinoceros.

Once the glasses hit the floor, Skyler began wailing as if mortally wounded, which touched off panic in the entire Primary. Suddenly the entire row of Sunbeams were screaming for their mothers.

Sister Browning bent down and picked up Skyler's glasses and tried to comfort him. When order was restored, she made Billy sit next to her and she watched him stick out his tongue at the chorister.

"Billy, I'm sure you've got a wonderful voice," she said to him.

Yeah, right, I thought. Billy's voice sounded like a bathtub full of wet cats.

"Won't you please sing the songs with us?" Sister Browning coaxed him.

"Okay," Billy said with a sneer. Then he shouted over the sound of everyone else singing:

I looked out the window and what did I see?
The new teacher attacked by a giant bee.
The sting brought her such a terrible surprise
Blood coming out of both of her eyes...

That was his way of welcoming Sister Browning to our ward, I suppose. But Sister Browning was unfazed. She was, after all, a professional teacher. She simply smiled and said, "You've got a way with words. You're quite the poet, Billy."

Yeah, a regular Edgar Allan Poe.

Then Sister Browning did something *really* strange—she put her arm around him. Billy immediately knocked her arm away. "Don't ever touch me, or I'll sue!"

"I'm sorry," Sister Browning said.

When we got to class, Sister Browning asked us to take our seats.

"Where do you want us to take them?" Billy asked.

Instead of telling him to stop being sarcastic, like most teachers did, Sister Browning smiled again. "Billy, you've got a good sense of humor."

Sister Browning, I decided, was *too* nice.

Then she asked each of us to stand in front of the class, one at a time, and tell her a couple of things about ourselves.

Skyler was first. This kid was seven going on 47. He attended a private school—partly to avoid Billy—and he talked like one of the adults. Maybe that was because he was the youngest of four kids and the next youngest child in his family was ten years older than he was. Two of his older brothers attended Harvard or Yale or some fancy-pants Ivy League school like that. Skyler always talked about going there himself.

The Cherringtons lived in a large, lavish home in an affluent part of town. From a young age, I dreamed of being as rich as the Cherringtons, living in a mansion and owning a boat and a fancy car, like they did. Skyler's dad was a lawyer. I had no idea what a lawyer was, but for a long time I thought it was another word for "rich."

"My name is Skyler Alexander Cherrington. When I grow up, I want to be an actor, a marine biologist, and a brain surgeon."

"Good," Billy spouted, "you can start by doing brain surgery on yourself."

"Oh yeah?" Skyler said. "You're the one who needs brain surgery. I bet you had to repeat *kindergarten*!"

"Boys," Sister Browning said, "let's not talk that way in church, okay?"

"I'm taking karate lessons and I have a green belt," Skyler continued.

Personally, I think Skyler's parents enrolled him in karate classes so he could defend himself against Billy Blankenship. Not that it did much good. Billy routinely pinched, punched, punctured and pummeled Skyler. His parents encouraged him to "turn the other cheek."

"Why?" I heard Skyler say, "so Billy can hit me on that one, too?"

Skyler's parents, like the rest of us, just hoped the Blankenships would eventually move away and become some other ward's migraine headache.

"I can beat anyone in chess and I get an allowance of $5 every week," Skyler droned on. "I take accordion lessons every Tuesday afternoon and I've won three straight regional spelling bees."

"What a nerd!" Billy shouted.

"When I was seven, I lost two teeth in one day," he said. "The tooth fairy left a $10 bill under my pillow!"

We all gasped. The tooth fairy only left me a measly dime when I lost a tooth.

"I bet your teeth fell out because you were eating so much," Billy said. "I bet you have to go to Fat Camp again this summer."

"Billy, let's not talk like that," Sister Browning said. "It's your turn."

Billy stood in front of the class. Before he could speak, Skyler couldn't resist taking a jab at him. "When's the flood coming?" he said, referring to Billy's pants, which hovered well above his ankles.

"Who cares, four eyes," Billy said. "When there *is* a flood, people will think you're a beached whale."

"Billy, please tell us something about yourself," Sister Browning said.

"I can drink a whole gallon of milk in two minutes flat," Billy said.

"Liar!" Skyler said. "Nobody can do that."

"That's quite a talent, Billy," Sister Browning said.

"That's nothin'. I can swim faster than anybody here. Someday, I'm going to win a gold medal in the Olympics."

Skyler laughed.

"I'm going to the beach later on today," Billy said. "Then my dad's taking me to a swap meet."

"Oh," Sister Browning said.

"We're not supposed to go to the beach on Sunday," Skyler said. "We're supposed to keep the Sabbath Day holy. You're not supposed to do anything fun on Sunday."

"That's neat that you can spend time with your dad, Billy," was all Sister Browning said.

After we all introduced ourselves, Sister Browning announced, "This is a very important year in your lives. Do you know why?"

Skyler's hand shot straight up in the air, just like it did for every question the teacher asked. I think Sister Browning was hoping someone else would have the answer.

"Todd?"

"We'll be going into sixth grade?"

"That's true," Sister Browning said, "but there was something else I was thinking of."

"Kevin?"

I knew the answer she was looking for, but I didn't dare say anything. If I did, there was no telling what Billy might say or do. I didn't want to subject myself to Billy's ridicule. So I just shrugged my shoulders.

Sister Browning glanced at all the other boys and they had blank looks on their faces. Skyler kept his arm up until it looked like all the blood had drained from his fingertips.

"It has to do something with the fact you're all turning 12 this year," she hinted. Still nothing. Billy was rocking back in his chair, pointing his finger at Sister Browning and making machine-gun noises.

A little frustrated, Sister Browning finally turned to Skyler, who looked like he was going to explode. "Why don't you tell us why this year is special for everyone in the class," she said.

Skyler cleared his throat. "It's because we're going to receive the priesthood. Actually, it's the Aaronic Priesthood, or the lesser priesthood. It's the power to act in God's name. We can pass the sacrament, collect fast offerings and be the bishop's messenger."

"Yes, Skyler, you're right. For young men, receiving the priesthood is one of the most important things you can do in this life. How many of you are looking forward to receiving the priesthood this year?"

Every hand went up, except for Billy's, of course.

"Look, Sister Browning," Skyler said, "Billy doesn't want the priesthood. He can't get it anyway. He does all sorts of bad things. I know where kids go who don't keep the commandments."

All the boys stared at Billy.

"So do I," Billy said. "The beach!"

"Oh, now," Sister Browning said, "I'm sure Billy wants to be a priesthood holder. Don't you, Billy?"

"No, I don't. And nobody can make me."

"You're right, nobody can make you," Sister Browning said. "It's something we have to be worthy to receive. Someday, when you're ready, you'll be able to receive that sacred power. It's power that comes through being obedient and serving others."

"That doesn't sound like any fun."

"But it *is* fun, once you understand it all," Sister Browning said. "I see you someday serving a mission, teaching people the gospel."

At that point, I wondered about Sister Browning. Either she wasn't a very good judge of character or else she was clinically insane. Billy Blankenship? A missionary? I was surprised Sister Browning wasn't struck down right then and there for such a ridiculous statement.

In the span of about 15 minutes, Sister Browning had complimented Billy five times, exceeding all of the other teachers' compliments to Billy over the years by, well, five. I wondered what my mom would think of all this.

Just before the end of class, Sister Browning called on me to offer the closing prayer. While we folded our arms and closed our eyes, Billy got down on the ground and tied my shoelaces to a chair.

CHAPTER 3

Skyler's Spectacles

I was glad, and relieved, when I saw Sister Browning back the following week to teach us. Of the dozens of Primary teachers we had over the years, she was my favorite by far.

She began class by allowing us to say one thing that happened to us during the week. "After that," she said, "it's my turn to teach the lesson. I would ask that you listen for the rest of the time, okay?"

With that, Billy flipped his eyelids inside out and leaped out of his chair. "Gross!" a couple of kids chorused.

"Billy," Sister Browning said, "did anyone ever tell you that you've got handsome green eyes?"

Billy just looked at her for a moment, somewhat stunned by that reaction. Nothing seemed to rattle Sister Browning.

"No," he said.

We all looked at Billy's eyes. Sister Browning was right; his eyes were a nice shade of green. I don't think any of us had ever noticed. None of us had ever dared look him directly in the eyes before, kind of like the way you're not supposed to look directly into the sun.

"You are a boy of many talents," Sister Browning said to Billy. "I can do that, too."

Then she flipped her eyelids inside out. I think Billy was a little annoyed. It was the first time he had been upstaged by a teacher.

"Teachers shouldn't do that," Skyler whispered to me. "I'm going to tell my mom. You should tell your mom, too."

After Sister Browning put her eyelids back in place, she looked down at her fingers, which had turned black. "I've got mascara all over me," she said. "Let me run to the bathroom. I'll be back in a minute."

While she was gone, Billy started rummaging through Sister Browning's bag.

"You're not supposed to do that!" Skyler protested. "I'm telling!"

"Shut up, you big fat blob," he said. "I can do whatever I want." He removed a pack of gum, unwrapped three or four pieces and shoved them in his mouth as quickly as he could.

"If anyone says anything," he said while chewing, "I'll stick a piece of bamboo through your fingernails."

"Bamboo isn't indigenous to southern California," Skyler said.

"You're no genius, either," Billy said, removing a knife from his pocket. "How would you like this in your ear drum?"

Nobody said a word. We all knew Billy was fully capable, without compunction, of sticking a knife through an ear drum.

Billy put his knife back in his pocket just as Sister Browning returned to the room. The only thing you could hear was Billy chomping madly on a pack of gum.

"Did someone get into my bag?" she asked, picking up some of the contents that had spilled onto the table.

Everyone except Billy looked around the room nervously.

"Who got into my bag?" Sister Browning asked again.

"I did!" Billy blurted out, relishing the attention.

"Did you take something?"

"Yeah!" he boasted. Billy opened his mouth, which held a massive wad of slimy gum.

Instead of getting upset, Sister Browning smiled. "Thank you for telling me the truth," she said. None of us could believe it. Billy swipes some gum out of the teacher's bag and he receives another compliment? What was wrong with this woman?

"If there's one thing I hope you'll learn this year, it's to be honest," Sister Browning added. "A worthy priesthood holder is always honest."

"Aren't you mad at him for what he did?" Skyler protested. "He broke the commandment, 'Thou shalt not steal.'"

"No, I'm not mad," she replied. "Billy, you shouldn't take things that don't belong to you. But, do you know what? Heavenly Father loves us no matter what we do. As your teacher, I love you, too."

I don't think anybody had talked to Billy that way before. Billy just sat there, glaring at Sister Browning.

"How could you love me?" he finally said. "You don't even know me."

"Well, I'm planning to get to know you as your teacher this year. I know you are a child of God. He loves you. No matter what you do, He will always love you."

Even Billy didn't have a sarcastic comeback for that. He just sat in his chair with a scowl on his face.

Before Sister Browning continued with the lesson, Skyler raised his hand.

"Guess what, Sister Browning? My family's going to Disneyland next week."

His family was always going to theme parks or taking exotic vacations to Europe. The only place my family ever went on vacation was Utah to visit relatives. It was never very exciting.

"You better not get on 'The Pirates of the Caribbean,'" Billy said, "because you'll make the boat sink."

"You're just jealous because you don't have enough money to go to Disneyland," Skyler huffed.

"Who cares about Disneyland? I get to go to the beach and to swap meets with my dad. Disneyland is for losers."

"Oh yeah?" Skyler said. "Your dad is the loser! He's a one-armed hippie!"

None of us knew much about Billy's dad, but we did know that he had fought in the Vietnam War and had one of his arms amputated after sustaining an injury.

"You better stop talking about my dad like that," Billy said. "He's a hero! He got the Purple Heart!" Then he quickly snatched Skyler's glasses right off his nose.

"Give me back my spectacles!" Skyler said. "You're getting your grimy fingers all over the lenses."

"Billy, please give Skyler's glasses back to him," Sister Browning said.

Billy started bending the glasses back and forth and a lens popped right out on the floor. Skyler gasped. "You're going to be in big trouble with my dad. Those cost $79.99, with tax."

"Like I care, four eyes," Billy said. As Sister Browning tried to intervene, Billy slammed the glasses against the wall, cracking the other lens and breaking the frames.

Skyler's bottom lip began to quiver. Then he pulled out a monogrammed handkerchief and began crying. "You broke my spectacles!"

At the time, that was one of the worst things I had ever seen Billy do—and that's saying something. Then again, what Skyler said to Billy was cruel, too.

I was curious how Sister Browning would handle the situation.

"Do you still love me *now*?" Billy asked her.

"Yes, Billy," said Sister Browning, who was on her hands and knees, picking up the pieces of Skyler's glasses and placing them on a table, "I do."

"Well, *I* don't love him," Skyler said, adjusting his bow tie. "I wish Billy wouldn't come to church anymore. Aren't you going to do something about this, Sister Browning? My spectacles cost a lot of money."

"Skyler, I'm sorry about your glasses," Sister Browning said. "I'll talk to your parents after class."

Skyler turned to Billy. "You're definitely not going to go to the celestial kingdom, like me."

"So what? I already told you that I hate Disneyland."

"Billy, you need to talk to your mom and dad about what you did to Skyler's glasses," Sister Browning said.

"No, I don't. My mom and dad don't care what I do. I can do whatever I want."

"Then I'll have to talk to your parents about what you did. Billy and Skyler, you owe each other an apology."

"Why do *I* have to apologize?" Skyler asked. "Look what he did to my glasses!"

"But you said something very unkind about Billy's dad."

"Everything I said about Billy's dad is true," Skyler sniffed. "I'm not apologizing."

Sister Browning took a deep breath, opened up the Book of Mormon, handed it to Billy and asked him to read a couple of verses.

"I'm not reading anything out of this stupid book," he said, then dumped Sister Browning's scriptures onto the floor.

With amazing calmness, Sister Browning bent down next to Billy. "This book is very special to me and what you did was disrespectful to me and to the Lord. Do you realize that many people suffered and died so we could read this book?"

"Like I care," Billy said.

"Well, *I* care. Now, will you please pick up the book?"

Billy continued glaring at Sister Browning. He slowly picked up her scriptures and handed them back to her.

"Thank you," she said.

"Is it time to leave yet?" Billy asked.

"Not yet," Sister Browning said. "Billy, you've got a strong personality. One day, you'll make a great leader."

We all looked at Sister Browning like she had lost her mind. *Leader?* A leader of what? An organized crime ring or a motorcycle gang? *It's great to encourage him like that, but let's not go overboard,* I thought. What in the world did she see in this kid?

I'm sure Billy was disappointed that Sister Browning didn't lose her temper like most of our teachers did. Not only was Sister Browning sweet as chocolate mousse, but she was also tougher than a three-dollar T-bone steak. That's a pretty strong combination.

Maybe Billy had met his match.

CHAPTER 4

The Impossible Assignment

Because my mom was the Primary president, she had to get involved in the situation with Skyler's broken glasses. Sister Blankenship apologized to Skyler's parents for what had happened, and, though the Blankenships didn't have much money, she offered to pay for new ones. Brother and Sister Cherrington knew that Billy's dad was a disabled army veteran and that Sister Blankenship was the breadwinner of the family, working five days a week as a secretary at the school where Sister Browning taught.

Besides, Skyler's parents were wealthy, so they accepted her apology and declined the offer.

The Cherringtons bought their son a new, and better, pair of glasses—which Skyler made us aware of as often as he could. Skyler's new glasses included an elastic band that fit snugly around his head so Billy couldn't knock them off anymore.

That same week, my mom called all of the parents of the kids in our Primary class to let them know about the annual Priesthood Preview, a special night for the 11-year-old boys and their parents to attend a meeting in the chapel and feast on a veal-and-vegetables meal in the cultural hall.

Billy's birthday was in June, but all of us knew he would never hold the priesthood. I was hoping he wouldn't attend the activity and ruin the occasion for the rest of us.

There was a knock on the door not long after Mom hung up

the phone with Sister Blankenship. It was Sister Blankenship, and she seemed upset. My mom invited her in and they sat down in the living room. Mom told me to go brush my teeth, but I was curious, so I sat in the hallway where they couldn't see me, and I listened to their conversation.

"I'm afraid Billy won't be attending the Priesthood Preview," Sister Blankenship sobbed.

"Why?" asked my mom, who was probably relieved. "Does this have anything to do with Skyler's glasses?"

"That's part of it. But mostly it's Eddie, my husband. Maybe you're not aware that Billy isn't even a member of the Church. He hasn't been baptized. He turned eight in our old ward and my husband refused to let him be baptized."

I didn't know that, but it made perfect sense to me. Billy didn't know anything about the Church or the scriptures.

"My husband was baptized when he was eight and he thinks he was too young to make such a serious commitment," she said. "In fact, he doesn't want Billy attending church anymore."

"Maybe I could talk to the bishop," my mom said.

"No, you can't! Eddie would be very angry with me if he even knew I said anything to you about this. I don't want the bishop involved, okay?"

"I'll respect your wishes, but I really think you should talk to Bishop Sweeten. He might be able to help."

"I've always dragged Billy to church against his will," said Sister Blankenship. "He's never liked church. On the day he was blessed, he screamed the entire time so that you couldn't even hear the blessing. When Billy was in nursery, he pushed kids down and stole their snacks. I don't think he'll ever change. And I don't think Eddie will ever let Billy get baptized. Maybe it's for the best that he stops going to church now. I don't see much point of him attending the deacons quorum if he's not even baptized."

When I heard Billy wouldn't be coming to Primary anymore,

I thought the ward should throw a parade. Church without Billy sounded good to me. It was bad enough that I had to spend Monday through Friday with him at school.

Sure enough, for the next three weeks, Billy didn't attend church. I overheard a couple of Primary teachers tell my mom that opening exercises had never been so peaceful.

While the Primary teachers and the Primary presidency—not to mention all the kids—were happy that Billy wasn't coming to church, Sister Browning seemed concerned.

One week she told us a parable from the Bible. She said Jesus told his disciples that if a man had 100 sheep and one of them wandered away, he would leave the 99 others to find the lost one, and when he found the lost sheep, he would be happier about that one than having the other 99. It sounded like a nice little story. I thought I'd probably feel the same way if I had lost one of my prized baseball cards.

After Primary, Sister Browning pulled me aside as the rest of the kids left the classroom. I thought I was in trouble for something.

"Kevin, you're a great example," she said. I could feel my face turning bright red. " I really appreciate how reverent and attentive you are every week in class."

I practically melted when she said that. Sister Browning had a way of making you feel good about yourself, which was one more thing I really liked about her.

"Thanks," I said. "If I'm not reverent, I don't get any dessert after Sunday dinner."

Sister Browning chuckled, then said, "You've probably noticed that Billy hasn't been at church for a while."

"Yeah." I wanted to say that it was kind of nice without him.

"You're in Billy's class at school, right?"

"Yeah."

"Do you ever play with him?"

"No. Nobody does."

"Do you ever talk to Billy at school?"

"Not if I can help it. One time Rusty Philmont asked Billy to pass him the scissors and Billy threw them right at his head. Rusty had to have stitches."

"Well, you know how important it is that Billy receive the priesthood, right?"

I nodded. "Doesn't he have to be baptized first?"

Sister Browning was caught off guard. "You mean he hasn't been baptized yet?"

"No. I heard his mom tell my mom that his dad wouldn't let him."

Sister Browning looked pensive for a moment.

"Well, you know that Jesus wants him to be baptized. Can you think of a way we can help Billy come back to church so he can be baptized, then receive the priesthood?"

I thought for a moment. Truthfully, I didn't want Billy back at church. But I knew better than to say that. I thought about the story Sister Browning had told us about the lost sheep. I don't think anyone other than her had thought of him as a lost sheep, but rather a lost cause.

"I guess Billy is like one of those sheep that Jesus taught us about," I said. "Maybe I could try to be his friend."

A tear rolled down Sister Browning's rosy cheek. Why, I wasn't sure. "Would you be willing to do that?"

"I guess so," I said uneasily. How could I say no to those soft blue eyes?

"I think Billy just needs a good friend," she said. "He just needs to feel loved and appreciated. Billy could turn out to be a really good kid."

I didn't see it myself. I wondered if she was talking about the same Billy Blankenship that I knew.

"He has so much energy bottled up in him," she added. "If

only we can channel that energy into doing good . . ."

Then Sister Browning said she was proud of me. "The Lord is, too. He will help you. Ask for His help, and you can be one of the Lord's shepherds. Let me know how it goes at school, okay?"

"Okay," I said as I left the classroom. I couldn't believe how much trust she had in someone like me, an ordinary 11-year-old kid. Didn't she realize what she was asking—to be Billy Blankenship's friend—was impossible? Let alone helping him get baptized and receive the priesthood.

Though I was scared, I knew deep down it was what the Lord wanted me to do. I decided at that time not to tell anybody, not even my mom and dad, about this assignment. That way, when I failed, no one would know, other than Sister Browning. But I promised her to do my best.

The next day, from the moment I woke up, my heart was beating hard as if I had some big spelling test that I hadn't studied for. I offered a special prayer the night before, asking Heavenly Father for help, so, at the least, Billy wouldn't beat me up. I knew that trying to befriend Billy would be hazardous to my health.

I kind of hoped he wouldn't be at school that day and, for a while, it looked like he wasn't going to show up. Billy eventually came traipsing into class 10 minutes after the bell, wearing a black T-shirt with a skull and crossbones on it. I took a deep breath.

During reading time I couldn't concentrate on my book. I kept looking at Billy, who was scribbling pictures of monsters on his shoes with a pen. He never could sit still. He regularly flunked his spelling and math tests. Not that he cared. I don't think he even tried at all, because failing was what was expected of him. He was labeled as a dumb kid, and most kids treated him that way, too.

Anyway, I knew I couldn't just walk right up to Billy and

say, "Billy, do you want to be friends?" He probably would have punched me in the kidney and waited for me to deposit my lunch on the ground.

I spent the entire morning thinking about what I might say to him. But nothing came to my mind.

Several days went by before I mustered enough courage to approach him. I knew Sister Browning was going to ask me about it, so I decided I'd better do *something*. I thought about doing something nice for Billy. But what? I remembered that I had one of mom's delicious homemade cupcakes in my lunchbox. I knew Billy loved sugar. Come to think of it, that may have been the root of his hyperactivity issues.

When I walked into the lunchroom, I found Billy sitting alone, as usual, with his tray of food, seeing how far he could spit his milk out with a straw. Sometimes he liked to make milk come out his nose, just to get a reaction out of people.

I sat beside Billy and he looked at me with disdain.

"Who said you could sit here? This table is saved for cool people."

I glanced at the otherwise empty table. I swallowed hard and thought of Jesus and Sister Browning.

"Can't I just sit here?" I asked.

"Why?"

"Well, my mom packed me a lot of food today, and I have a chocolate cupcake that I won't be able to eat. It's really good."

Billy must have thought it was all some sort of trick by the way he was looking at me. I dug into my lunch sack, removed the cupcake and handed it to Billy.

"Here," I said. "Hope you like it."

Billy took it and examined it all over. Then he sniffed it.

"Yuck!" Billy exclaimed. "That smells horrible!"

"What do you mean?" I said. "I thought you liked chocolate."

"Chocolate?" Billy replied. "I don't think this is chocolate. It looks like something else. Smell it to make sure."

I leaned forward to smell the cupcake. Just as I breathed in, Billy shoved the cupcake into my face, covering me with chocolate frosting from my forehead to my chin.

As I wiped chocolate out of my eyes, Billy laughed and pointed his finger at me.

"Look at him!" he exclaimed as other kids also began to laugh at me. "You look like you just fell into a pile of manure!"

Then he stood up, dumped his tray of food into the garbage and ran out to recess, laughing all the way.

Humiliated, I found a napkin in my sack that mom always packed for me but I never used. For the first time in my elementary school career, I used it. I cleaned my face the best I could, trying not to let anyone see me cry.

Is this what I got for trying to be one of the Lord's shepherds? I wished I had never taken on that assignment from Sister Browning.

"Are you okay?" one of the lunch ladies asked me.

"Yeah," I said.

"What happened?"

"I, uh, made a little mess."

"Do you need any help?"

"No thanks."

I didn't feel much like eating after that, so I threw away my lunch and slunk outside to the playground. All those good feelings I had about Billy when I had prayed for him the night before had disappeared.

Then I remembered Jesus and how He was nice to everyone, even those who were mean to Him. I remembered how my parents taught me that people spit on Him and put a crown of thorns on His head and nailed Him to a cross. Compared to that, a chocolate cupcake in the face wasn't *that* bad.

Besides, I knew that I couldn't give up that easily. I also knew that if Billy were ever going to change, it would take a major miracle.

Sister Browning had told us the story about Alma in the Book of Mormon. Alma was worried about his son, Alma the Younger, who was a problem child that reminded me of Billy Blankenship. Alma prayed and prayed for help from Lord to reform his son. The Lord answered his prayer by sending an angel to scare Alma the Younger into repenting.

So I prayed that Heavenly Father would send an angel to Billy and tell him to start being nice. I figured that's what it would take for Billy to change and be able to be baptized and receive the priesthood. This much I knew: I couldn't complete Sister Browning's assignment alone.

CHAPTER 5

The Valentine's Day Incident

Sure enough, the following week Sister Browning pulled me aside and asked me how it was going with Billy.

"Um, not so good," I said, staring at my shoelaces.

"Well, I'm praying for you," Sister Browning whispered.

For a couple of days I went back to ignoring Billy. That approach had worked for years. Luckily, he left me alone. But my promise to be Billy's friend kept gnawing on my conscience. Plus, I knew Sister Browning, and the Lord, were counting on me.

During recess I spotted Billy sitting alone near the playground, throwing rocks at some kids playing hopscotch. I had a basketball in my hands and I decided to walk right over to him. My friends couldn't understand why I would have anything to do with Billy, especially after what he did to me with my mom's cupcake.

Before I could say anything to Billy, he said something to me.

"What do *you* want?"

"I just wanted to know if you wanted to play basketball with me."

He looked at me strangely, probably because nobody had offered to play with him before. "I don't play basketball with losers like you," he said.

"If you change your mind, I'll be shooting baskets over there."

Dejected, I began to walk away when he called me.

"Hey, kid," he said. "Come back here."

All those years we were in the same Primary and school classes, and he couldn't even call me by name. I went back, not sure what he was going to say, or do, to me.

"You look like a kid from church," he said, studying my face.

"I *am* from your church. We're in the same ward. I'm Kevin Russell."

"Oh, yeah," he said. "You're one of those goodie-goodies. Well, I don't go to church anymore."

"Why?"

"Because it's boring and dumb. Church is for losers. My dad and I go to games and swap meets and the beach on Sundays. It's a lot more fun than going to church."

To be honest, those things *did* sound like more fun than going to church.

"Do you have any balloons at home?" he asked me.

I thought that was a weird question.

"I think so. Why?"

"Bring 'em to school tomorrow," he ordered.

I wanted to ask why, but I didn't. It could have been worse. He could have asked me to bring a chain saw or rat poison. Maybe he wasn't allowed to play with balloons at home. It seemed like a harmless request.

"Okay," I said.

"Don't forget," he added, "or I'll rearrange your face with my fists."

All the rest of the day I wondered if we really did have any balloons at home. And if we didn't, I wondered how I would get them. I didn't want to suffer the consequences if I didn't produce them.

After school I went straight home, finished my homework and practiced the piano. Mom was in the kitchen baking heart-shaped cookies. The next day was Valentine's Day.

"Mom, do we have any balloons?" I asked.

"Yes, why?"

Before I could answer, mom said, "Oh, your classroom party is tomorrow. I'll put them in your backpack with your Valentine cards."

That was easy enough. True, we were going to have a classroom party, but no one had said anything to me about bringing balloons.

At school the next day I excitedly showed the balloons to Billy as soon as I saw him.

"Don't show them to everybody, dummy," he whispered. "Bring them out at lunch. Meet me outside by the garbage bins."

I told him I would. He was actually talking to me in what was, for him, a civil tone. I was making progress. I thought about how proud Sister Browning would be of me.

All the kids in our class brought homemade Valentine's Day boxes—except for Billy. When I asked him why, he replied, "Because it's stupid. Love and hearts are stupid."

Later, I overheard a couple of kids say they were glad Billy didn't have a box because they weren't going to give him a Valentine anyway.

As planned, we met on the playground. I carried a bag of balloons under my shirt. He quickly grabbed them from me and threw them into his empty backpack. Then, with a devious smile, he said, "Follow me."

My instincts told me that following Billy Blankenship anywhere wasn't a good idea, but in this case, it seemed like the right thing to do. I was being his friend, after all. Isn't that what Jesus would have done?

Billy went back into the school and slipped into the boys' bathroom. I followed.

"Block the door," he demanded.

I did what he told me to. I stood in front of the door and watched him pull out the balloons and fill each of them with water from the faucet. Within a few minutes, he had about a dozen water balloons in his backpack. I had a bad feeling about it, but I was already in on his scheme pretty deep.

"What are you going to do with those?" I asked.

"You'll find out next recess."

That kept me guessing for the next couple of hours. I knew it was something sinister, but what could I do? I was an unwitting accomplice.

When the bell rang he told me to follow him. He led me to the back of the school and, with his backpack on, he jumped onto the giant metal garbage bin, then grabbed hold of a small ladder that hung from the wall. He lifted himself onto the roof of the school.

"C'mon. Get up here!" he said.

"I don't think we're supposed to climb up there," I said. Did I mention I was afraid of heights?

"What are you, a chicken?"

"Maybe," I said.

Billy mocked me. "Ask any Mermaid you happen to see, 'What's the best tuna?' CHICKEN of the Sea!"

Against my better judgment, I carefully climbed up onto the roof with Billy. I nearly slipped and fell into the garbage bin.

"Hurry up, you wimp!" Billy called.

From on top of the roof we walked to the opposite side, looked down, and saw hundreds of kids playing below. My stomach felt a little queasy, either because of the heights or because I realized what Billy was going to do with those water balloons.

He removed all of them from his backpack and set them down by his feet. He crouched down, picked up a big blue one, wound up, and launched it through the air like a catapult. The balloon nailed a girl right in the leg, splattering water all over her. She began screaming.

Billy laughed, admiring what he had done, and tossed another balloon, dousing some kid's shirt. I just stood there, not knowing what to do, while kids throughout the playground yelled and frantically ran for cover.

Another water balloon hit a boy, almost knocking him down. Yet another drenched a girl's fancy red Valentine's Day shoebox decorated with lace and hearts.

Suddenly we saw Principal Luginbill storm out of the school, searching for the culprit. Billy threw a balloon that struck Principal Luginbill on top of his shiny, bald head.

Ducking low, Billy scurried across the roof to the other side and climbed down. I stood there, frozen. By the time Principal Luginbill figured out where the balloons were coming from, he looked up, rubbing the top of his soaked skull, and spotted me, sheepishly standing alone on the roof.

"Get down here, right now!" he yelled at me.

When I climbed down, Principal Luginbill was waiting at the bottom. He grabbed me by the back of the neck. "You come with me, young man," he said. "What is your name?"

"Kevin Russell," I said.

"Well, Kevin Russell, you just earned yourself a month of detention. As soon as we get to my office, I'm calling your parents. I don't know what kind of a stunt you were trying to pull, but I should probably expel you from school!"

Everything happened so fast that I didn't know what to say. I had never been in trouble like this. I had never seen the inside of the principal's office before.

Of course, Billy was long gone. He had devised an escape plan and didn't bother telling me about it. He was in trouble so often, he knew how to handle these kinds of situations. I didn't. What would my parents think when they found out? What would they do to me? I figured I'd probably be grounded until my mission.

Principal Luginbill had one of the teachers, Mr. Robinson, climb the roof and bring the unused water balloons down as evidence.

"Do these balloons belong to you?" Principal Luginbill asked.

"Yes, sir," I said.

The principal shook his head. "I can't believe it. This is something Billy Blankenship would do," he muttered under his breath. "Did he have anything to do with this?"

"No, sir."

Around the faculty lounge, I learned later, the prank was referred to as the "Valentine's Day Incident."

Now, I knew I could get myself out of this mess simply by telling Principal Luginbill and my parents the truth. I could honestly say that it was actually Billy's idea and that he had perpetrated the crime.

Despite the consequences of taking the blame, I couldn't bring myself to tell on Billy. I decided to leave him out of it. I knew that if I told on him, he would never trust me or ever want me to be his friend. Then he would never go back to church, or get baptized, or get the priesthood. And it would be my fault. Certainly, I thought, the Lord would understand if I protected Billy.

Principal Luginbill called my mom at home and told her what had happened. She told the principal she didn't think her son was capable of such a thing and that he must be mistaken. She called my dad, who left work right away and arrived at the school.

When my parents showed up, I was sitting outside the principal's office, nervously tapping my foot.

"Kevin," said my mom, who was on the verge of hyperventilating, "is what the principal told us true?"

I frowned. "Yes. I'm sorry."

"You mean that's why you wanted those balloons I gave you yesterday?"

"Yes."

Mom looked at me as if she didn't recognize me. "How could you do something like this?"

"Your mother and I are very disappointed in you," my dad said. "What do you have to say for yourself?"

"I'm really sorry."

"You won't be allowed to play with friends or ride your bike for a month," my mom said.

Because it was my first offense, Principal Luginbill sentenced me to a week of detention, rather than a month. That meant I had to stay after school every day and clean up the classrooms and the playground.

Everyone stared at me when I returned to class that day. They were stunned that I would throw water balloons from the school roof.

I noticed that Billy just kept looking at me out of the corner of his eye. I'm sure he was surprised that he didn't get called down to the principal's office, too.

When the teacher left the room, Billy confronted me and, instead of being grateful for not tattling on him, he acted very suspicious.

"Did you say anything about me to Principal Loogie?"

"No," I said.

"Why not?"

Billy seemed a little disappointed, as if I were taking all the credit for his evil actions.

"That's what friends do."

"Since when are we friends?"

"Since today," I said. If I was going to be grounded and go to detention, it wasn't going to be in vain.

Late that night as I got out of bed for a drink of water, I

overheard my mom and dad having a serious conversation about me. "What are we going to do with Kevin?" my mom asked.

I felt terrible and wished I could tell them what really happened.

"Maybe it's just a stage he's going through," Dad said.

"I'm the Primary president," Mom said. "I can't have my son acting like this. He's always been such a good kid. Am I not spending enough time with him? Did we miss some signs? None of this makes sense."

Because of Billy, my parents were mad at me and my friends distanced themselves from me. I hoped that the Lord and Sister Browning, at least, appreciated all I was trying to do to help Billy Blankenship.

CHAPTER 6

Eddie Blankenship

Just because I took the blame for Billy—and went to detention and was grounded, all because of him—didn't mean that he suddenly acted like I was his friend or anything.

Billy continued to do bad things at school, but at least he had the decency to leave me out of them. I tried to encourage my friends to include Billy at recess, but they said I was crazy. If I was going to be Billy's friend, I'd have to do it alone. Every day I greeted him when he got to school and invited him to play with me at recess.

A couple of weeks after the Valentine's Day incident, after my detention was over, he invited me over to his house. I was a little scared because I had never been there before. Mostly, I was scared because of Billy's dad.

I didn't tell my parents where I was going. They never would have approved.

Once I entered his house I discovered one of the reasons why Billy talked so loud. Rock 'n' roll music blared from a radio that practically shook the house's foundations. I couldn't figure out how anyone could think clearly with the music cranked up to ear-shattering decibels.

"My dad likes this kind of music," Billy yelled to me, though we stood two yards apart.

Billy led me to his room, an asylum of squalor. Dirty socks, mud-caked rocks and candy wrappers covered the floor. On the wall was a poster of Farrah Fawcett of *Charlie's Angels* fame. I immediately averted my eyes.

One of the few things we had in common was an affinity for baseball cards and we compared our collections. While we were looking at our cards, Billy's dad burst into the room wearing tight bell-bottom Levis and a tie-dyed shirt. He was a strapping man with broad shoulders. Long, stringy brown hair hung in his face in front, and in the back it was tied in a pony tail, dangling past his waist. His face was covered in a thick beard that could have served as a nest for a family of swallows.

It was hard not to notice his missing right arm. He staggered toward us. I was terrified.

"What are you doing?" Billy's dad asked in a hoarse voice, waving the stump of his left arm at us. His eyes were bloodshot and his breath reeked of alcohol.

"Looking at baseball cards," Billy said.

"Who are you?" Billy's dad asked me.

"I'm Kevin Russell. I'm Billy's friend."

Billy's dad just stared at me for a minute. "I didn't know Billy had a friend."

It was easy to see where Billy inherited his charm.

"We're in the same class at school and in church," I added.

"You're a Mormon?" he asked.

"Yes, sir," I replied.

"I don't like Mormons," he said.

"Well, *you're* a Mormon," Billy said to his dad. His dad kicked the door and stomped out of the room in a huff.

I had heard bits and pieces about Billy's dad over the years, how he had fought in the Vietnam War and had only one arm.

I wished I had never met him.

"That was scary," I told Billy.

"Oh, that's nothing," Billy said. "He does that all the time. I'm used to it. At least he didn't hit me."

"Your dad hits you?"

"Yeah, sometimes. Only after he's been drinking. That's why I'm never going to drink alcohol. Not because some church tells you not to. Because I can see it does bad things to people."

That was encouraging to hear.

"My mom says he gets mad sometimes because he was in the Vietnam War. He can't really help it. He was shot a few times and he lost his arm and they gave him some cool medals. My mom says he hasn't been the same since. He doesn't ever want to be around me."

"I thought you said he takes you to the beach and to football games and swap meets on Sundays," I said.

"I just made that stuff up. I just ride my bike, swim, or sit in the house and watch TV on Sundays. My dad never takes me anywhere. But don't tell anyone."

After seeing a glimpse of what Billy had to deal with at home, I started to understand why he acted the way he did. It occurred to me that all of those bumps and bruises that Billy had weren't from doing stunts, like he'd say. I felt bad about judging him so harshly all those years.

"Does he hurt your mom, too?" I asked.

"Sometimes. But you better not ever say anything, okay?"

"Okay. I won't say anything," I said. "Are you ever going back to church?"

"My dad says I don't have to," he said. "So I'm not going anymore. Church is boring and a waste of time."

I felt like I had failed.

The following day at recess, Billy shoved me for no apparent reason. "Hey," he said, "do you have anything to eat? Like a candy bar?"

"No," I said. "My mom usually won't let me eat candy bars. Unless Sister Browning gives them to me."

"Who's Sister Browning?"

"You know. Our Primary teacher."

"She gives you candy bars?"

I knew this was my chance.

"Oh, yeah," I said. "Every time we pass off an Article of Faith, she gives us a candy bar. If we memorize all 13, she'll take us to buy a milk shake."

"Is it a big candy bar like the ones the rich people give out for Halloween, or one of those dinky ones that cheap people give out?"

"The big ones," I said. "I can even help you learn the first Article of Faith and you can go to church on Sunday and pass it off to her. And you'll get a candy bar. It's really easy."

"You better not be lyin' to me," Billy said.

"I'm not. It's the truth," I said.

"What do we have to memorize?"

"There are 13 Articles of Faith. They were written by Joseph Smith, the prophet. They say what we believe. The first one is, 'We believe in God, the Eternal Father, in His Son, Jesus Christ, and the Holy Ghost.' If you tell that to Sister Browning on Sunday at church, she'll give you a candy bar."

Billy was quiet for a moment. "I don't think I can memorize anything."

"What do you mean? You have no trouble memorizing TV commercials."

"Well, maybe I'll come to church this week, just to get my candy bar," he said. "You sure the teacher has one for me?"

"Yeah."

"Will you help me learn that one?"

"Sure."

"I'll come to church if you make sure I get a candy bar. She better bring it, or I'll crack your head open with a baseball bat."

Billy sure was creative with his threats.

"Okay," I said. Whatever it took to get him back to church. I spent the rest of recess teaching him the first Article of Faith.

I figured Sister Browning would be so proud of me. So I called her house that afternoon and told her that Billy would be coming to class on Sunday. She seemed really excited and told me to tell Billy that she would have a candy bar for him.

CHAPTER 7

The Deaf Kid

I found out from my mom that someone else would be in our class that Sunday, a new kid that had just moved into our ward.

"His name is Danny Rayford," she said as she fixed a tuna casserole. "His dad's in the military and he's been transferred here. Danny's a very special boy."

"What do you mean by 'very special'?" I asked.

"Well, he can't hear."

"He's deaf?"

"Yes. I'd like you to make him feel welcome and be his friend on Sunday. Can you do that?"

I said I'd try.

"His birthday is in December, like you, so he'll be receiving the Aaronic Priesthood when you do. I talked to Danny's mother today and I think she's nervous about how he'll be accepted by the other kids. There have been problems in the past . . ."

"Uh-oh," I said.

"What?"

"Billy's going to be at church this week."

"How do you know? I thought you said he wasn't coming to church anymore."

"Well, today he told me he's coming."

"What changed his mind?"

"I told Billy about how Sister Browning gives us candy bars for memorizing the Articles of Faith."

Mom seemed worried about him returning to church and disrupting Primary, and I couldn't blame her. Who knew what Billy might do to a deaf kid? Knowing what he did to Skyler's glasses, I could only imagine what he might do to a boy with hearing aids.

"I want you to sit by Danny in class and protect him from Billy," my mom said. "We can't have any problems."

So Sister Browning wanted me to be Billy's friend and my mom wanted me to be Danny's bodyguard. I wondered if it were possible to do either, let alone both at the same time.

At church, before Sister Browning arrived, Billy found his way into the classroom.

"Why did *you* come back to church?" Skyler asked him.

"I came here to get my candy bar, fatso," Billy said. "After I get it, I'm out of here. And I'm not ever coming back again."

"Good!" Skyler replied. "But you're too dumb to memorize any of the Articles of Faith."

"Oh yeah?" Billy said. "'We believe in God the Eternal Father and in His Son, Jesus Christ, and in the Holy Ghost.'"

"Very good, Billy," said Sister Browning as she entered the classroom. "It's good to have you back with us."

Then she patted his shoulder. "We've really missed you."

"You owe me a candy bar."

"You're right," Sister Browning said, handing him a Snickers bar out of her bag.

As Billy ripped off the wrapping and stuffed half of the candy bar in his mouth, the new boy, Danny, the one with hearing aids in both ears, walked in, accompanied by his mother.

Everyone fell silent as they gazed at Danny, who didn't make eye contact with anyone. He looked shy and frightened.

"This is Danny Rayford," Sister Browning said. "He's new to our ward and we'd like to welcome him to class."

On cue, Billy spoke up, with a mouthful of chocolate. "What's wrong with *him*?" he asked, with caramel trickling out of the side of his mouth.

Danny's mom looked like she was going to cry.

"As you may have noticed, Danny can't hear," Sister Browning said.

"You mean he's deaf?" Billy blurted out.

"Let me tell you about Danny," Danny's mom said. "He hasn't been able to hear since he was born. We didn't realize that until later. He is about 85 percent deaf in both ears. As you can see, he wears two hearing aids, which are very expensive. That allows him to hear some sounds. He doesn't talk very well. Mostly he communicates by reading lips and through sign language."

"What's sign language?" asked Billy.

"It's his way of communicating. Instead of words, he uses symbols he makes with his hands. Danny's father and I have learned sign language, too. It has its own alphabet."

Then she went through the first several letters of the alphabet with her hands.

I looked over and Billy was trying to imitate Sister Rayford.

"Danny goes to a special school with other kids who can't hear," she explained. "But he'll be coming here every week to church. Danny's dad is in the military and we've had to move a lot. Danny has a hard time making friends because we don't stay long in one place. But he is eager to make friends with all of you."

We went around the room and introduced ourselves to Danny by saying our names. Sister Rayford signed each of our names and Danny looked at his mom, then at us, to put a face with each name.

"Thank you, Sister Rayford," Sister Browning said. "Now let's go on to our lesson."

Sister Rayford remained in front of the class, using sign language to translate everything for Danny. None of us were really listening to Sister Browning. We were all watching Sister Rayford's strange hand signals. Billy seemed fascinated by the whole process.

"Hey," he asked Sister Rayford, interrupting Sister Browning, "does Danny watch TV?"

"He doesn't watch much TV," she answered. "He mostly reads."

"What if the fire alarm goes off and everyone hears it but him?" Billy said, sounding a little worried. " He'd get stuck in a building and burn to a crisp."

"Then someone would have to help him," Sister Rayford said. "But I have a feeling if there were a fire, Danny would be the first one to notice."

"How?" Billy asked.

"While Danny can't hear, his other senses are very good."

"What do you mean?" Billy asked.

"Danny notices smells and sights that we either take for granted or don't notice at all. He appreciates life and the world's beauties in a different way than we who can hear do. He's good at reading lips. Danny doesn't listen with his ears, he listens with his eyes and his heart."

"Cool," said Billy.

"Danny isn't as different from you and me as you might think," Sister Rayford continued. "He likes to play games, read books, and eat ice cream. He does many things that you do. He's excited about getting the priesthood this year. Someday he hopes to go on a mission."

"How can *he* go on a mission," Billy said, "if he can't hear?"

"Like I said, he communicates in other ways," Sister Rayford said. "He writes very well and he gets good grades in school. There are other people in the world like him who can't hear and he can teach them the gospel in sign language."

"Does it make him mad that he can't hear?" Billy asked.

"No, he's not mad about it," Sister Rayford said. "I'm sure he would like to be able to hear, but Heavenly Father made him that way. He understands that."

"Do kids ever make fun of him?" Billy asked.

"Yes, some do," Sister Rayford said. "Some tease him and trick him. A couple of years ago he came home from school crying almost every day. That's why we put him in a special school with other kids who can't hear."

"What kind of tricks did they play?" Billy asked.

"They've taken his hearing aids, which are *very* expensive," she said.

"I'd beat up anyone who did that to him," Billy said.

I think everyone was shocked when he said that. Sister Rayford smiled.

"How do you say 'hello' in sign language?" Billy asked.

Sister Rayford opened her right hand and waved it back and forth several times. Billy did the same.

"How do you say 'friend' in sign language?" Billy asked.

Sister Rayford interlocked the right and left hands at the index fingers. Then she separated them and brought them together again.

None of us who knew Billy could figure out what had gotten into him. We had never seen him actually take an interest in anything or anyone, but he was riveted to his seat.

"So he can't hear music?" Billy asked.

"Danny doesn't hear music," Danny's mom said. "He *feels* music."

"How?"

"He can put his hand on a radio and feel the beat."

While Sister Rayford and Billy were talking, I noticed that Danny didn't seem very happy. He looked mad, though I wasn't sure why.

After about 10 minutes of Billy's question-and-answer

session with Sister Rayford, Sister Browning continued with her lesson. All of the sudden Danny began babbling incoherently, communicating something to his mom, though we couldn't understand anything he said. He sounded very frustrated and he furiously made symbols with his hands.

"Danny just said he would like me to leave. He likes to be independent," Sister Rayford explained. "It was nice meeting all of you."

She signed something to him before walking out the door. Billy couldn't take his eyes off Danny.

"If there is a God, why would He make it so Danny can't hear?" Billy demanded to know.

"What do you mean, Billy?" Sister Browning asked.

"If God loves us, like you say He does, why would He make it so Danny can't hear? Why would He let my dad get his arm shot off? That's not fair."

"Billy, those are excellent questions," Sister Browning said, opening her Bible. "Once, Jesus' disciples asked him a similar question." Then she read, *'And his disciples asked him, saying, Master, who did sin, this man, or his parents, that he was born blind?*

"Jesus answered, Neither hath this man sinned, nor his parents: but that the works of God should be made manifest in him."

"What's that supposed to mean?" Billy said. "I hate scripture-talk. It doesn't make any sense."

"Listen carefully to the words," Sister Browning said, then read the passage again. "What do you think Jesus was saying, Billy?"

He sat quietly for a minute or so—quite possibly a personal best—lost in thought. "Like I told you. I don't know," he said.

"I think it means that all of us came to earth with special talents and special challenges," Sister Browning said. "Some of those talents and challenges are easier to notice than others. With Danny, it's something that we notice because most people can hear. Danny can help us appreciate that we can hear. I'm sure he can teach us many things. Why don't you think about it and when we come back next week, we'll discuss it."

Did I mention that Sister Browning was smart?

For the rest of the lesson, Billy sat quietly, staring at Danny. Afterward, Billy did something that surprised us again. Looking at Danny, he interlocked the right and left hands at the index fingers. Then he separated them and brought them together again.

"Hey, I'm your friend," Billy said loudly.

Then he took Danny by his sleeve and looked him in the eyes. He proclaimed very loudly and slowly, so Danny could read his lips. "Come . . . with . . . me . . . I'll . . . take . . . you . . . to . . . your . . . mom."

Danny nodded and followed Billy. I wondered if Billy was really going to take him to the girls' bathroom and lock him in a stall. But I followed them and, sure enough, he found his mom in Relief Society.

"Thank you," Sister Rayford told Billy. "You're such a nice boy."

CHAPTER 8

Danny's World

For some reason, Billy was obsessed with Danny. Maybe, I thought, it was because Danny was disabled, like his dad.

A few days after we met Danny, Billy asked me if I knew where he lived.

"Yeah," I said. "Why?"

"Let's go play with him after school."

"I can't. I'm grounded."

"Grounded? For what?"

I couldn't believe he was asking me that. "For the water balloons. *Remember?*"

"Oh," Billy said. "When will you not be grounded anymore?"

"Next week."

"Okay. Next week let's go to Danny's house."

To me, that didn't sound like much fun. How are you supposed to play with a kid you can't talk to? But Billy was determined. I wasn't worried so much about Billy teasing Danny, but, knowing Billy, he had a knack for stirring up trouble. Nobody knew that better than I did.

During the week I hoped Billy would either forget about Danny or lose interest in the whole idea. But he didn't. The next week he started pestering me about it again.

"We don't know when his school is, or if he is allowed to play," I said.

"Let's go over there today," he insisted.

When I got home from school I asked my mom if I could ride my bike to Danny's. My sentence for the balloon incident was over, and she said it was okay. I met up with Billy down the street, and from there we pedaled to the Rayfords' house. We knocked on the door and Sister Rayford answered.

"Hi, boys," she said, looking surprised to see us.

"Is Danny here?" Billy asked.

"Yes, he is," she said.

"Can he play?"

"You want to play with Danny?"

"If that's okay," I said.

"Why, sure. Come on in. He's reading right now."

She led us through the living room and into the kitchen, where Danny sat at an oak table. He didn't notice us at first. His nose was buried in a thick book. Next to him sat a plate of peanut butter cookies and a big glass of milk.

Sister Rayford touched Danny on the shoulder and he looked up. He smiled at us, grunted, and excitedly motioned for us to sit down. We did and Sister Rayford brought cookies and milk for us, too. Billy swallowed his glass of milk in one gulp. Then he wiped the milk off his mouth with his sleeve and burped.

"What . . . are . . . you . . . reading?" Billy asked Danny slowly and loudly.

Danny handed him the book. Billy handed it to me.

"*The Red Badge of Courage* by Stephen Crane," I said, reading the cover. Billy grabbed the book back from me and flipped through the 170 pages.

"Hey," he said, "there aren't any pictures."

Then he turned to the first page and squinted at the words. He looked at me and said, "Read this."

So I did. "*The cold passed reluctantly from the earth, and the retiring fogs revealed an army stretched out on the hills, resting.*"

"What is this book about?" Billy asked, interrupting me.

"It's about the Civil War," Sister Rayford said.

"Cool. I love war stories," Billy said. "With blood and guts and machine guns."

"There were no machine guns at the time of the Civil War," Sister Rayford said.

"What's the Silver War?" Billy asked.

Sounding like a school teacher, Sister Rayford explained things like "the North and South," "slavery," "Emancipation Proclamation" and "Abraham Lincoln."

"He's reading about *that*?" Billy said.

"Danny loves to read," Sister Rayford answered, pointing to the bookshelf. "He loves the classics."

My eyes scanned the shelf, which included *The Adventures of Huckleberry Finn, Call of the Wild,* and *20,000 Leagues Under the Sea*.

I realized that even though Danny couldn't talk, he was very intelligent.

"What else does Danny like to do?" Billy asked.

"He got a science kit last Christmas," Sister Rayford said. "Would you like to see it?"

"Yeah," Billy said. "Can you blow stuff up with it?"

Sister Rayford signed something to Danny, who took us to his bedroom. On the wall was a poster of the solar system, a map of the world and the periodic table of the elements.

"This kid's like Albert Einstein," I whispered to Billy.

"What grade is Albert in?" Billy asked me.

"Never mind," I said.

Danny showed us his erector set, his ant farm, his science kit and his marble collection.

There was something I still couldn't figure out: why Billy was so interested in Danny. They seemed to have nothing in common.

I finally told Billy my mom probably wanted me home, so we said goodbye.

"Thanks so much for coming over, boys," Sister Rayford said. "You're welcome anytime."

For days after that, Billy couldn't stop talking about Danny, how he wished he went to the same school we did. Later, on his own, he went to the Rayfords' house and started learning from Danny's mom how to communicate simple words and phrases in sign language.

"It's like a secret code," Billy told me. "It's like being in the CIA."

He and I would try to communicate in sign language with Danny and I think Danny appreciated the effort, though most of the time we got the signs wrong. At least we made him laugh as we tried to communicate, usually unsuccessfully. We invited Danny to our houses to play, but Danny's mom wouldn't let him. "It's best that you play here with him," Sister Rayford said.

Maybe it was because of Danny, or maybe it was the candy bars that he earned after I helped him memorize the Articles of Faith, but Billy started attending church again. Billy was Danny's self-proclaimed protector.

During Primary, Sister Browning asked a question and Danny raised his hand. She called on him and he responded by making grunting sounds no one could understand.

"How can he answer a question?" Skyler scoffed. "He can't even talk."

Billy stood up and got in Skyler's face. "Don't ever talk about Danny that way. You don't know anything about him. He's a lot smarter than you."

"He's not smarter than me," Skyler said. "He's deaf."

I thought Billy was going to deck Skyler. But Sister Browning brought calm to the situation. Billy signed to Danny that everything was fine. Danny then signed something to Billy.

"Danny says that he needs to go to the bathroom," Billy said.

None of the kids could believe that Billy was actually defending someone, let alone communicating in sign language.

When we played at Danny's house, his mom hovered over us and doted on Danny constantly. I could tell Danny was bothered by his parents' tendency to be overprotective of him. Though he couldn't speak clearly, his facial expressions made it easy to know exactly what he was thinking. He wanted to do things on his own, like other kids.

Danny kept a notebook filled with pages and pages of poetry that explained his feelings. Billy had me read the words to him. Many of the poems were about what it was like to be deaf. His only wish in life was to be able to hear, to be treated like a normal person. He hated the way people stared at him and thought of him as being "weird." He had feelings, like everyone else. Billy and I wanted to help him feel like a normal kid.

Looking back, I guess Billy and Danny did have a lot in common. They both felt like misunderstood outcasts. Danny, I think, was someone Billy could relate to. It was kind of an unlikely friendship, but in some ways, it made perfect sense. Danny was the kid who couldn't hear. Billy was the kid who couldn't listen.

It was Danny's turn to read a scripture during opening exercises of Primary. He had volunteered to do it and I wondered how that would work since it was so hard to understand him when he tried to speak. Danny's mom came in with him and she stood off to the side while Danny walked up to the podium.

He held his scriptures in his hands, but he didn't open them. Most kids read from their scriptures, but Danny had memorized his. When he opened his mouth and started quoting the scripture, the words sounded like gibberish. Determined, Danny pressed on, blabbering into the microphone. Soon almost all of the kids started giggling uncontrollably.

Billy wasn't one of them. He looked around the room like he wanted to lay waste to anyone who was making fun of Danny. "Everyone be quiet!" Billy shouted. "Just because he can't hear or talk very well doesn't mean he's dumb. He's smarter than all of you put together."

It wasn't the way my mom would have handled that situation, but I think she appreciated what he said because everybody stopped laughing.

Sister Rayford strolled to the podium and put her arm around her son.

"Danny wanted to share his favorite scripture with you," she said. "It's Third Nephi 17:7. This is Jesus Christ speaking to the Nephites after His resurrection. It says, *"Have ye any that are sick among you? Bring them hither. Have ye any that are lame, or blind, or halt, or maimed, or leprous, or that are withered, or that are deaf, or that are afflicted in any manner? Bring them hither and I will heal them, for I have compassion upon you; my bowls are filled with mercy."*

Then Danny's mom removed a tissue from her purse and dabbed her eyes.

Danny looked at his mom and started signing to her. "Danny wants to tell you that this is his favorite scripture because he knows that some day, because of Jesus Christ, he will be able to hear. He says these things in the name of Jesus Christ, amen."

Billy elbowed me in the ribs. "Could Jesus really do that? I mean, make Danny hear?" he asked me.

"Yeah, he could. He did all kinds of miracles, like walking on top of water. He even brought dead people back to life."

"No way."

"It says so in the Bible."

"If Jesus is dead, how can He still do miracles?"

"Jesus isn't dead," I explained. "He was resurrected. He's alive."

"He's *alive*?"

Even though I knew Billy never paid attention in Primary, it surprised me that he didn't know that. It was news to him.

"You mean He can do miracles *now*?" Billy asked me.

"My mom and dad say He can."

"Do you think that's true?"

"Yeah."

"You mean he could bring my brother back to life?"

I didn't know Billy had a brother. "You have a brother?"

"Yeah. He died when he was a baby. Could Jesus bring him back to life?"

I didn't have an answer for that question.

"Well?" he demanded.

"I guess He could if He wanted to. I bet someday you'll be able to see your brother, in heaven."

Billy just searched my eyes for a moment, as if to make sure I wasn't joking or lying, then he glanced at the large, framed picture of Christ at the front of the Primary room.

I could only wonder what was going through his mind.

CHAPTER 9

Aquaphobia

We had an interesting mix of boys in our Primary class. Billy and Skyler were on opposite ends of the spectrum. Everybody else was somewhere in between.

There was nothing particularly special about me, and I kept my mouth shut for the most part. Being the son of the Primary president, I had some pressure to always be well-behaved and reverent. Not that it was too hard.

Sister Browning had gotten the idea to hold a class party, and she thought it would be nice to hold it at Billy's house on a Saturday afternoon. Billy had a pool in the backyard and Billy's mom thought it would be great for the kids to swim and have a barbecue. The home originally belonged to Sister Blankenship's mother. When she got old, the Blankenships moved in with her. Sister Blankenship's mother had died a couple of years earlier.

Danny's parents wouldn't let him attend our Primary party. "Danny's not a very good swimmer," they said.

I wasn't a very good swimmer, either. In fact, I had spent several years living in fear of water.

Like most kids, I was excited to get baptized. When you grow up in the Church, getting baptized is something you do almost automatically. It's simply expected. But when I was six, something traumatic happened that changed me.

Even though I grew up in southern California where swimming pools were commonplace and where we were a short bike ride from the Pacific Ocean, I suffered from an acute case of aquaphobia. I learned that word when Skyler got it during one of his spelling bees that my mom made me attend. He asked the judge to give the word's definition.

"It means 'a morbid fear of drowning.'"

When I heard that, my ears perked up. I didn't know there was an actual word that described how I felt about the water.

Skyler then spelled it perfectly. A-Q-U-A-P-H-O-B-I-A. I never forgot that word.

Let me explain. The summer after I turned six, my family and I were at the beach, having a great time. While my parents and brothers and sisters were playing volleyball, I sneaked off by myself down the shoreline and waded into the ocean. I was mesmerized by the ebbing and flowing of the white-crested waves. I wanted to see how far out I could go. As I ventured into the water, suddenly, a powerful undertow dragged me under. It was as if an invisible force had grabbed me by the ankles. I floundered under the water, suffocating and panicking before I was able to break free from the water's grasp. Once I did, I pulled myself to the shore. I coughed up salt water and sand. Out of breath, and shaken, I returned to my parents.

"Kevin," my mom said, "what's wrong? You look pale."

I told her what had happened. I had violated a family rule—never go swimming alone.

She told me never to do that again, and I told her I wouldn't. That experience had a lasting impact, though. My near-drowning experience haunted me. When I went swimming with my family after that, I tried to hide my fear the best I could.

I finally told my parents about my fear of the water and they were understanding. It made me feel better to talk about it.

On my baptism day, my turn to step into the font arrived. My heart was beating fast. I took a deep breath and my dad took my hand. He held it firmly and led me into the cool water. When we got in far enough, I gripped my dad's wrist with my right hand. I held on tightly. But when I closed my eyes, something funny happened. Everything went calm. All I could think about was Heavenly Father and the promise I was making with him. I listened carefully to the words of the prayer, then I plugged my nose and bent my knees, just as my dad had told me to.

Before I knew it, I was under the water for an instant, then I came back up. My dad and I hugged each other.

That day, my fear of water disappeared. I decided I wanted to be a great swimmer, though at the time I wasn't very good.

I took swimming lessons for a while, but when my older brother stopped taking lessons, my mom made me stop, too. I wished our family had a swimming pool. I decided that when I grew up, I'd make enough money to buy a swimming pool.

CHAPTER 10

The Pool Party

At the pool party, Billy effortlessly swam lap after lap after lap. I was impressed. I had fantasized about being an Olympic swimmer and winning a gold medal.

Sister Browning never got into the pool; she just watched us from the side. "Billy, you are a terrific swimmer," she said. "How did you get so good?"

"I just swim a lot," he said.

"He practically lives in this pool in the summer," his mom explained.

That day, for the first time, I realized Billy's talents extended beyond guzzling milk and belching. When it came to his swimming prowess, I would have sworn that he really was bionic.

Billy could hold his breath for a long time under the water and some of the kids would throw a penny in the bottom of the deep end and he would go down, pick it up and emerge from the water, holding the penny aloft. When he swam laps, his legs kicked furiously yet evenly and his strokes were pure and coordinated, barely making any splash in the water. It was as if he were part dolphin.

Skyler arrived late because, he said, he had spent the morning at a water treatment plant to receive extra credit for some report. When Skyler removed his "spectacles," he asked Sister Browning to watch them for him.

"Don't let Billy touch them," he said.

Skyler removed his T-shirt, revealing his white and prominent stomach. Billy laughed and put on a pair of sunglasses.

"You're going to blind us all," he said.

Billy jumped off the diving board and did a cannonball into the pool. "You better not do that," Billy told Skyler when he came to the surface, "or we'll all drown."

Sister Browning and I went into Billy's house to help bring out some of the food for the barbecue.

"These paintings are beautiful," Sister Browning said to Billy's mom, admiring a picture of a beach at sunset hanging on the kitchen wall. "Where did you get them?"

"My husband painted them," she said.

We were both surprised. I don't think anybody knew he was an artist. Who could have known that a man with such a hardened exterior could have a soft, sensitive side?

Down the hallway there were more paintings, one of Sister Blankenship in her wedding dress, and one of Billy when he was very young.

"Did he paint all of these?" Sister Browning asked.

"Yes," Sister Blankenship answered. "But he did those a long time ago. He hasn't painted in years."

"He has a real gift," Sister Browning said.

That's when Billy's dad staggered out of a room and looked at us suspiciously. He was shirtless and his hair hung in his face.

Sister Browning didn't care. She said hello to him. "These paintings are wonderful. You know, I have a cousin who is a talented artist. I tried to draw with her, but I never could. I really admire those who can paint like this."

Billy's dad did not respond. He simply walked to the refrigerator, pulled out a can of beer and popped it open. Then he walked outside to where all the kids in our Primary class were playing and started swilling the beverage.

"Look!" Skyler said. "Billy's dad is drinking beer! I'm going to tell my mom about this!"

I could tell Billy was humiliated. He kept on swimming, acting like he was oblivious to the whole thing.

Sister Blankenship came out of the house. "Eddie, come inside, won't you? Let the children swim."

"Are you telling me what to do?" Billy's dad roared.

"No, Eddie. I just think . . ."

"Stop thinking. This is my house," Billy's dad yelled, waving his stump in the air. "I want all of you Mormons off my property!"

"What are you staring at?" he screamed at Skyler, who started to cry.

"Kids," Sister Browning said, comforting Skyler, "I think it's time for us to go."

While we all grabbed our towels and hurriedly put on our shirts and flip-flops, Billy's dad walked toward the edge of the pool and started yelling incoherently at Billy while the rest of us got out of there.

Alcohol consumption and a domestic dispute. It was some Primary party.

CHAPTER 11

The Stolen Pencils

A lot of the kids at my elementary school collected football pencils. We had a pencil machine by the principal's office that sold them for 10 cents each. Each pencil featured the colors of a National Football League team and the name of that team engraved in small letters on the side.

Though Skyler didn't go to our school, he told us he had a complete set. Except he didn't buy his one at a time. He bought in bulk. When he saw other kids trying to collect them, he had his dad buy a full set for him and he kept them in a glass case at home. Funny thing is, Skyler didn't even like football.

I was proud of my collection and I never sharpened those pencils so I could keep them in pristine condition. Whenever I earned some money, I'd pay my tithing, then I'd take whatever was left over and go down the hall at school to the pencil machine, put in a dime, push the metal lever, and await my pencil, hoping for one I didn't already have. I got a lot of duplicates. After a while, I needed only two more for the complete NFL set—the Miami Dolphins and Minnesota Vikings.

For some reason, I had a hard time getting those two pencils. I told Billy about my dilemma.

A few days later our teacher, Mr. Dent, started class by talking about respecting other people's property, and how it was wrong to ever take something that did not belong to you from someone's desk.

"Eric told me this morning that two of his football pencils are missing from his desk," Mr. Dent said. "He's very upset about this. Does anyone have anything to say about it?"

"Which football pencils are they?" someone asked.

"The Miami Dolphins and the Minnesota Vikings," Eric said. "I marked them with my initials on the erasers."

I thought it was a coincidence that those were the two pencils that I needed to complete my set. I had unsuccessfully tried to trade him for his Dolphins and Vikings pencils a few weeks earlier.

I slowly opened my desk and peered inside. As I looked at my collection, my heart sank when I saw a Miami Dolphins pencil and a Minnesota Vikings pencil. On the erasers were Eric's initials.

I knew I hadn't taken them, but I couldn't figure out how they wound up inside my desk.

"Would someone like to tell me and the class what they know about this?" Mr. Dent asked.

My heart was beating fast. Finally, I raised my hand.

"They're here in my desk," I said.

"Kevin, did you take Eric's pencils?" Mr. Dent asked.

"No, I didn't," I said.

"Then why do you have them?"

"I don't know."

"Those are the only two pencils he needs for a full set," Eric said. "Kevin stole them!"

"No," I said. "I didn't. Honest."

I looked across the room at Billy, who was sitting quietly at his desk, looking at the ceiling. I picked up the two pencils and returned them to Eric. "I'm sorry," I said, "but you have to believe me that I didn't take them."

"I don't believe you," Eric said.

During recess, Mr. Dent talked to me about it.

"Is it possible that you really wanted those two pencils badly because you were frustrated about not being able to get them on your own?"

"No, Mr. Dent. I didn't take them. I promise."

"Then who did?"

"I don't know."

"Kevin, I'm getting worried about you. First the water balloons, now this. You used to be a model student. I think we ought to walk down to the principal's office and call your parents."

As we made that long walk to Mr. Luginbill's office I thought about how I used to win citizenship awards in school.

The secretary looked up my home number in my file and handed me the phone.

"I want you to tell your parents what happened," Mr. Dent said as he dialed my number.

I knew my dad was at work. I was hoping my mom would be out shopping or something. Instead, she answered.

"Hello?"

"Hi, mom."

"Kevin? Why are you calling? Are you okay?"

I told her the story with Mr. Dent standing there, breathing down my neck.

"Mom, you believe me, don't you?"

There was brief silence on the other line. "Yes, I believe you," she said. "But that doesn't explain how those pencils got in your desk."

Then she spoke to Mr. Dent for a while. I wasn't sure how I was feeling. Here I was, trying to find Billy, the lost sheep, and all I kept finding was trouble.

At recess I asked Billy about what had happened.

"Do you know how those pencils got in my desk?" I asked.

"Yeah. I put them there," he admitted.

"Why?"

"Because you needed them for your collection. You weren't supposed to tell anybody that the pencils were in your desk, dummy. Haven't you ever stolen anything before? Are you going to tell on me?"

I realized Billy's heart was in the right place, even though his hands weren't.

"No," I said. "I won't tell on you. But you have to promise to quit getting me in trouble. I can't keep taking the blame for you. I know you were trying to help me, but you went about it all the wrong way."

"Okay," Billy said.

"I'm getting ready to get the Aaronic Priesthood in December. I can't keep getting in trouble like this."

"Why do you want to get the priesthood so bad, anyway?"

That was a great question. I thought about that for a moment. "Well, we get to pass the sacrament on Sundays," I said. "And we get to collect fast offerings." Billy just stared back.

"And on Wednesdays, we get to go to Boy Scouts."

"What's that?"

The Scouting concept was foreign to Billy. From what I can recall, Billy went to Cub Scouts once, at Sister McKay's house. Billy intentionally ran over her Siamese cat in the driveway with his bike.

When she saw what had happened, Sister McKay began screaming hysterically and while running to retrieve her pet, she slipped and sprained her ankle. She went to the doctor and Precious was taken to the vet. Both of them were laid up for weeks.

Billy was never invited back to Sister McKay's house.

"We get to wear a uniform to Scouts . . ." I told Billy.

"Like an army uniform?"

"Yeah, sort of."

"My dad was in the U.S. Army. He wore a uniform. What else do you get to do?"

"We tie knots, use pocket knives, go camping and swimming. You can win awards."

"Awards? Like the Purple Heart?"

"I don't know about that, but I think you can get cool patches."

"Do I have to get the priesthood to be a Scout?"

"I think so," I said. Everyone I knew who was a Scout had received the priesthood first.

Billy frowned. "Do you have to be baptized to get the priesthood?"

"Yeah," I said.

He looked even more disappointed.

"What does Scouts have to do with church stuff?" he asked.

That was another good question. I didn't know how to answer that.

Later that night, I asked my dad if you had to have the priesthood to be a Scout. "No," he said. "There are other religious groups that have their own Boy Scout troops."

At school the next day, I told Billy what my dad had said. "Cool. I want to be a Boy Scout. I just don't want to do all that dumb church stuff."

CHAPTER 12

The BB Gun Incident

Billy owned a black and brown BB gun and he showed it to me when I was at his house. I thought it was really cool, especially since I knew my mom would never, ever let me have one.

I think Billy felt bad about the problems he caused me with the pencils, so he invited me over after school to see his gun again. He loaded it with BBs.

"It looks kind of dangerous," I said. "My mom said some kid in Kentucky lost an eye because he got shot with one of those."

Billy laughed. "Don't worry. I won't shoot people with this thing."

"What are you going to shoot?"

"There are a whole bunch of cats in the alley behind our house. Let's go!"

I guess Billy didn't like cats for some reason.

"Billy," I said, "my mom won't let me shoot cats. Or any other living creature."

"Your mom is sooooo boring," Billy moaned. "We can shoot something else."

"What?"

"C'mon," he said, "I'll show you."

So I followed him on my bike and we ended up at the church. He stopped and hopped off his bike. I got worried.

"What are we doing here?" I asked, knowing Billy didn't like going to church—especially not on a Friday afternoon.

"This is where I come for target practice," he said. "I'm a pretty good shooter."

"I don't think we should be here," I said. I didn't want to say it to Billy, but I was pretty sure the Lord didn't approve of firearms on the church grounds.

"Don't be a chicken," he said as he placed a few empty pop cans on a church window sill.

Billy counted off 30 steps. Then he turned, cocked his gun and began firing at that can. *Ping! Pang!* When he was through, he ran up to inspect the damage.

"Look at these holes!" Billy exclaimed, brandishing the gun in my face.

"Cool," I said, trying to act impressed. "Why don't we go to the park or something."

"C'mon!" he said. "It's your turn. Give it a try."

I had never even held a gun before, let alone shot one.

"It's easy," Billy said as he reloaded the gun. "You just put the butt of the gun on your shoulder, like this. Then you look through the crosshairs there on the barrel. You can't miss. When you line up your target, you squeeze the trigger. Like this."

Pop! Ping! Another can was demolished.

People in the ward predicted that Billy Blankenship would be in prison by age 15. The sight of him with that gun in his hand made it easy to see how that could happen.

"Um," I said as he handed me the gun, "I don't think my parents would allow me to do this."

"Your parents aren't here. They'll never know," Billy said. "Don't be a wimp. Just once. It's not going to hurt anything."

I gulped hard. "Okay. I'll shoot once. That's all."

Billy stepped behind me, ready to coach me through it.

My hands were trembling as I brought the gun up to my shoulder. I looked through the gunsights, but I couldn't hold it still because I was shaking so badly. I squinted and aimed at the can. Just as I was squeezing the trigger, Billy shouted right in my ear: "Aaaaaaaahhhhhhhhhggggggg!"

The sound scared me so badly that it caused me to jerk the barrel to the left.

Bam!

Next thing I knew, I had put a giant crack in one of the church windows. It was the window of the Primary room.

I dropped the gun on the ground and bowed my head in dismay.

Billy laughed. "Cool!" he said.

"No, it's not cool!"

I was mad at him for making me shoot the gun and I was mad at him for scaring me and causing me to break the window. Most of all, though, I was mad at myself. At age 11, I had committed an act of vandalism.

As we approached the window to check out the damage, a stern policeman approached us from behind.

"What are you boys doing?" he asked.

"I . . . I accidentally shot this window," I admitted.

"You're coming with me," the officer growled. He loaded my bike in the trunk of the police car and drove me to my house. At least he didn't turn on the sirens and lights.

You can probably imagine the look on my mom's face when we pulled up in the driveway and I stepped out of the car with an armed police officer.

"Kevin? Are you hurt?" Mom asked. "What happened?"

"Son," the officer said, "you had better tell you mother what you did."

"I accidentally broke a window at the church," I said.

"How?" Mom asked.

"With a BB gun."

"A BB gun!" she said, her face turning red with anger. "How would you get a gun? Who does it beong to?"

"It's Billy's gun," I said. "It was an accident. Really. It slipped."

"What have I told you about using guns? You know you're not supposed to play with guns. Didn't I tell you what happened to that boy in Kentucky? Let alone shooting at a church window."

Mom was so disappointed in me. I promised her I would pay for the window.

"You bet you will pay for it," she said. "Thank you, officer. That's the church we go to, so I'll talk to the bishop there so we can replace the window."

The officer nodded, got back into his car and drove away.

"Is this the kind of things you do when you're with Billy?" Mom asked.

"No," I said. "I won't do it again."

I spent the rest of the day confined to my room, grounded. I could hear my mom calling my dad at work. I overheard her say she felt like a horrible mother. "Where did I go wrong? I'm the Primary president and my son's a juvenile delinquent!"

My dad came home from work and talked to me for quite a while. He and mom came up with a new rule. "You are not allowed to play with Billy Blankenship anymore," my mom said.

"The way you've been acting, I don't know if you should get the priesthood," my dad said. "Your behavior the past few months has been unacceptable. First you throw water balloons at kids at school. Then the pencils. Now this. Your mom and I are so disappointed in you."

Those words broke my heart. "I'm sorry," I mumbled.

I prayed that my parents could understand everything. "Mom, I'm just trying to be Billy's friend," I said. "Billy has no friends, except for me."

Those words must have influenced my mom because she decided to give me another chance with Billy. I promised her there wouldn't be any more problems.

Still, Mom and Dad weren't happy about me spending so much time with Billy.

"It all comes back to the parents," Dad told Mom. "They're responsible for this. You let a kid do what he wants and of course he's going to walk all over you and turn into a wild animal."

"Don't be too hard on Billy's parents," Mom replied. "I think Billy likes to reject other people first, before they can reject him. It's sad. He's in for a very long and difficult life. We've got to help him the best we can. I'm glad Kevin is trying to be his friend, but you've got to draw the line somewhere. I don't want to put Kevin's future in jeopardy because of Billy."

I spent a lot of Saturdays pulling weeds and scrubbing the kitchen floor so I could pay for that window. As I worked, I wondered why it was so hard to help someone get baptized.

CHAPTER 13

Brother Woodson's Lesson

We entered the classroom at church and saw Brother Woodson standing there next to Sister Browning, smiling. He greeted each of us with a handshake.

When we sat down—Billy was between Danny and me—Sister Browning introduced Brother Woodson as the deacons quorum adviser. He was about the same age as Sister Browning, I guessed. He had returned from a mission and graduated from college. He wasn't married and lived with his parents. He owned his own business and drove a red Camaro. I really looked up to him because he was cool and had money. I wanted to drive a nice car like that someday.

"I've asked Brother Woodson to teach today because when you turn 12, you'll be going to the deacons quorum and he'll be your teacher," Sister Browning said.

"It's great to be here with you today," Brother Woodson began.

"Is this going to be boring?" Billy asked.

"That depends on you. If you listen and participate in the lesson, I promise you'll learn a lot. Today I'd like to talk to each of you about priesthood power."

"Power?" Billy asked. "Like the Incredible Hulk's power?"

"No, I'm talking about a much greater power."

"Like Superman?"

"No, God's power."

"Like when He parted the Red Sea or destroyed the Tower of Babel, right?" Skyler asked.

"Something like that," Brother Woodson said. "Worthy men, young and old, can receive a portion of God's power through something called the priesthood. When you turn 12, you can be ordained to the Aaronic Priesthood and become a deacon. With that priesthood, you can do things like pass the sacrament and collect fast offerings. And after you do that, God will give you more responsibility, or power, to do things like baptize, go home teaching, and give blessings."

"That doesn't sound like power to me," Billy said. "It sounds boring to me. I'd rather have power to blow things up."

"Well, Billy, the Lord doesn't want to destroy. He wants to build. It is through the priesthood that this world was created. The Lord wants you and me to become like Him. Everything He does is for our good. As holders of His priesthood, we are able to help Him. Priesthood is all about service. This priesthood power isn't for us to be able to brag about ourselves and look like we're better than others. It allows us to bless the lives of others. And when we do that, we receive blessings ourselves."

Just then, Billy shot a spit wad at the chalkboard.

"Please let's not do that at church," Brother Woodson said, cleaning the soggy mess off the board. Then he confiscated Billy's straw. "Billy, I don't know whether to slug you or hug you."

"Can I slug *you*?" Billy asked.

"Sure, after class," Brother Woodson said.

"Do you have to be baptized to get the priesthood?" Billy asked.

"That's a great question. Yes, you need to be baptized. Baptism is the first step we must take."

"Well, I'm not baptized, so I guess I can't ever get the priesthood."

"Do you want to be baptized someday?"

"I dunno."

"Let's talk a little about baptism, then," Brother Woodson said. "Who knows what baptism is?"

"I know the definition of baptism," Skyler said dramatically. "It derives from the Greek word *baptien*, which means 'to dip.'"

"*You're* the dip," Billy said.

"When we're baptized, we make covenants with Heavenly Father. Anyone know what a covenant is?" Brother Woodson said.

Skyler raised his hand. "It's a promise between two people. One person promises something and the other person promises something, too."

"Has anyone here made a promise with another person before?"

"Me!" Billy blurted out.

"Remember, Billy, you need to raise your hand," Sister Browning said.

Billy raised his hand.

"Billy?"

"I once made a promise with Raymond Tuttle at school."

"What did you promise?" Brother Woodson asked.

"I promised Raymond if he didn't give me his dessert at lunchtime, I'd punch him in the stomach as hard as I could."

"When we get baptized, we promise Heavenly Father that we will follow the Savior's example, keep the commandments, serve others, and be an example to others. Heavenly Father promises us that He will guide us and bless us. The Lord promises to forgive us of our sins so we can be clean."

"Fresh and clean as a whistle!" Billy called out, quoting an Irish Spring soap commercial.

"Who knows what happens after we are baptized?"

"We receive the gift of the Holy Ghost," Skyler said.

"Can anyone tell me what the Holy Ghost is?"

"A ghost with a bunch of holes in him," Billy shot back.

"The most important gift you receive when you get baptized you can't see or touch, but you can feel," Brother Woodson said.

"What's that?" Billy asked.

"The gift of the Holy Ghost. It's been the best gift I've ever received in my life. Heavenly Father promises us that when we get baptized, His spirit can always be with us, as long as we keep the commandments. The Holy Ghost helps us feel peace and happiness. It helps us in making decisions."

"How does the Holy Ghost do that?" Billy asked.

"The Holy Ghost is a spirit— he doesn't have a body. But we can feel his influence. When we have the Holy Ghost with us, he can bless us with the wisdom and courage to do what's right. Your baptism day is one you will remember all of your life. You should remember that date like you do your birthday. In fact, it's better than a birthday, because you get to celebrate it every week."

"Every week?" Billy asked.

"When we take the sacrament, we remember our baptism and we renew our covenants with Heavenly Father by eating the bread, which symbolizes the Savior's body, and the water, which symbolizes His blood."

"Oh," Billy said. "Eating birthday cake and ice cream and hitting a piñata full of candy is more fun than eating bread and water. Is it true that everybody has to be baptized to live with God?"

"Yes," Brother Woodson said.

"So my brother won't be able to live with God?"

"Your brother?" Sister Browning asked.

"Ricky," he said. "He died when he was a baby. One morning my mom found him in his crib and he wasn't breathing. My mom and dad were sad for a long time after that. My dad still is, I think. Ever since, he's been drinking a lot of beer. My brother was never baptized. So does that mean he can't live with God?"

"Billy, I'm so sorry that happened to your brother," Sister Browning said. "But do you know what? Your brother doesn't need to be baptized because he died before he was eight years old. The Lord tells us that those who die before the age of eight don't need to be baptized. So Ricky is already living with Heavenly Father."

"He is?" Billy asked.

"Yes."

"How do you know that?"

"I know because it says that in the scriptures."

"Where does it say that?" he asked.

Brother Woodson wrote down some scriptural references for him. "Why don't you go home and read these with your mom and dad and you can talk about these things."

"Well, I probably will with my mom, but my dad won't want to," he said.

"Are you sure?"

"He doesn't like church things. He doesn't want me to get baptized."

"Billy, do you want to be baptized?" Brother Woodson asked.

Billy looked around the room. Every eye was on him.

"If I do, will I be able to see my brother again?"

"The first step to returning to Heavenly Father is having faith, repenting and getting baptized," Sister Browning said.

"Why?"

"Let me give you an example," Brother Woodson continued. "Heaven is like a big, white house with white walls and white carpet."

"Sounds boring," Billy said.

"Like I said, this is just an example to help you understand the importance of baptism. To get into heaven we need to be clean and pure, like Heavenly Father is. Like your little brother is. When we're here on earth, we get dirty by making mistakes and not keeping all of the commandments. Imagine if you showed up to the door of Heavenly Father's beautiful house and you wanted so much to go inside, but you saw all of the white carpet and white walls. Then you looked down and saw that your shoes were covered in mud and your hands were filthy. What would you do?"

"That's easy," he said. "I'd just jump into my swimming pool and clean off."

"Right. You need *water*. That's what baptism is for—to wash away all your sins and to become clean again. Your brother never made any mistakes and is clean. To be with him, you need to be clean, too. That's why we need to be baptized. If we keep trying to follow Jesus, He has promised us that we can live together, forever, with our families."

A couple of days later, I realized Billy must have been thinking a lot about Brother Woodson's lesson. I think he must have felt something during it, too.

"Maybe I should get baptized," he told me. "Then maybe someday my mom and dad and me will get to see Ricky again."

CHAPTER 14

Let's Make a Deal

Sometimes Billy would do things to me, as if to test my loyalty, to see if I would still be his friend under any circumstance. While we were walking to the cafeteria for lunch the last week of school, Billy reached into my back pocket and grabbed my wallet.

It wasn't much of a wallet. It was brown and made of plastic. My older sister had bought it for me when she visited Tijuana and gave it to me for Christmas. I only had a few possessions inside it, like a couple of my favorite baseball cards, pictures of my family and some cash.

"Hey, what are you doing?" I asked Billy.

"I just want to see what's in your wallet."

"Don't," I pleaded.

Billy opened it up and passed over the pictures and baseball cards. But when he saw the crisp five-dollar bill inside, he gawked.

"Wow!" he shouted. "Five bucks! Where did you get that?"

When Billy said "five bucks," he said it very loudly so that everyone in the line turned to look at me.

"I'll tell you where I got it later," I said, taking my wallet away from him.

After lunch, we went to the playground. How I got that money wasn't a secret, but it wasn't exactly something I wanted to be common knowledge among the other kids in class.

"My mom and dad gave me this money a few days ago for

reading the Book of Mormon," I told him.

"How much did you have to read?" Billy asked.

"The whole thing, from cover to cover. There are more than 500 pages."

"Wow," Billy said in amazement. "Five hundred pages."

"My parents have done it with all my older brothers and sisters, too. If we read the entire Book of Mormon, they give us $5."

"How long did it take?"

"About six months."

"Did you really read it?"

"Of course I read it all," I said. "Every page. Every word."

"Did you understand it?"

"Not a whole lot," I admitted.

When my parents offered $5 to read the Book of Mormon, I was purely motivated by the money. The parts of the Book of Mormon I didn't understand, I just skipped over and kept on reading.

"What are you going to buy with your money?" Billy asked.

"Well, I've got to give 50 cents of it to the bishop for tithing," I said. "The rest is going to help pay for that window I broke at the church. My mom said I've got to spend summer vacation saving up enough money to pay for it."

"That stinks," Billy said. "Your parents sure are mean."

Then he asked if he could hold the money again. I opened up my wallet and handed it over.

"I wish I could get some money," he said. Billy raised the bill over his head and tossed it into the wind. I screamed in a panic and he laughed as he watched me chase it all the way from the swings to the monkey bars. When I finally caught up with it, I picked it up and carefully placed it back in my wallet.

"That was funny," Billy said.

"No, that wasn't funny," I said, almost out of breath. "I worked hard for that money. Why don't you ask your mom if she'll give you five dollars for reading the Book of Mormon?"

Billy got a crestfallen look on his face.

"What's wrong?" I asked.

"Nothin'."

"It's five whole dollars," I said. "Do you know what you can buy with five dollars?"

"Yeah. A new pocketknife." He paused. "Can you keep a secret?"

"Yeah," I said.

"Cross your heart, hope to die, stick a needle in your eye?"

"Cross my heart, hope to die, stick a needle in my eye," I repeated.

"I don't know how to read," he said, then looked at me as if he expected me to laugh at him.

Of course, I wasn't surprised Billy couldn't read. I had never seen or heard him read anything before. Whenever we read aloud, whether in Primary or at school, he always found a way out of it, usually by doing something to get kicked out of class. Every day at the same time he had to take a book from his desk and he would leave the class for an hour to meet with Mrs. Buttars, a resource teacher.

The only thing I had heard him spell was "Rolaids." You know, like the old TV commercial, "*R-O-L-A-I-D-S. Rolaids spells relief.*"

"I wish I could read," he said. "But it's real hard for me."

That was the surprising thing to me, that he *wanted* to read. I didn't think he cared about reading. I felt sorry for him and I wanted to help. Then I thought about how interesting it was that Billy didn't seem scared of anything, like heights or deep water. But he was scared of something simple—reading—that came so easily to me.

"Can *you* keep a secret?" I asked him. I couldn't believe I was actually going to tell anyone this—let alone Billy Blankenship.

At that moment, it didn't seem to matter that I didn't trust him hardly at all.

"Yeah," he said.

"Cross your heart, hope to die, stick a needle in your eye?"

"Cross my heart, hope to die, stick a needle in my eye."

"I'm not a very good swimmer."

Billy laughed. "You don't know how to swim?" he said. "You're almost 11 years old. I learned how to swim when I was three."

"I know how to swim, just not very well," I clarified. "I want to be a fast swimmer, like you. Why don't we help each other. I'll help you learn how to read if you teach me how to swim fast."

"Well, I'm the best teacher for swimming fast. I want to swim in the Olympics someday," he said.

"Me too!" I said. "We could train together."

"It's a deal," Billy said.

Then Billy spit into the palm of his hand and stuck it in front of me. That made me a little queasy, but I spit in my own hand and we shook on it.

School let out for the summer a few days later and I went to Billy's house to swim. My mom made me promise three things: that I would only swim when Sister Blankenship was home (she had most of the summer off from her job at the school), that I would stay out of trouble, and that I wouldn't touch Billy's BB gun. But I didn't tell her about my deal with Billy. I hoped that I could help Billy read the Book of Mormon so he could get baptized.

I was apprehensive about going to Billy's house, though, because of my previous encounters with Billy's dad. My mom warned me to stay away from him.

When Billy's mom got home from work she made us cookies and milk. She loved the idea of him reading the Book of Mormon. She loved it so much that she promised him if he read the entire Book of Mormon, she would pay him $50. I have to admit, I was a little jealous. I wished my parents would have paid me $50 for reading the Book of Mormon.

"I'm going to buy a new skateboard!" Billy said.

He was more motivated than ever and he couldn't wait to start. "Kevin, you make sure he reads it all," Billy's mom told me. "Okay?"

"Okay," I said.

We borrowed his mom's scriptures. Billy and I started with 1 Nephi 1:1, the verse where Nephi talks about his "goodly parents." That first chapter took more than an hour to read. He had a hard time sounding out letters. Sometimes, he mixed up the letters and I had to help him. He really stumbled over words like "nevertheless," "commencement," and "abominations."

"Why do they have to talk like this?" Billy said. "Why can't they just say 'you' instead of 'thou?'"

I didn't know the answer. "That's just the way they talked, I guess."

When we finished the first chapter, he told me he didn't understand a thing. I tried to explain things the best I could. As we'd read together, he'd ask me questions about certain stories and people in the Book of Mormon.

He liked the story about Nephi lopping off the head of Laban. He said he couldn't understand Laman and Lemuel. "Those guys are pretty dumb," he said. "An angel came down from the sky and got mad at them and they still didn't do what they were supposed to." I was encouraged that he didn't see them as the heroes and he correctly identified the good guys and bad guys.

"What did Sister Browning mean when she said people had died so we could have this book?" Billy asked me.

"Well," I said, remembering a recent Family Home Evening lesson, "in the Book of Mormon, there were the Nephites and the Lamanites. The Nephites believed in Jesus and the prophets wrote about Him on gold plates. The Lamanites tried to get the plates, probably so they could have the gold. At the end of the Book of Mormon, the Lamanites and the Nephites had a big war and all the Lamanites killed all of the Nephites. One of the last Nephites, Moroni, buried the plates in the ground to save them for the future, for us to read."

"Thanks a lot," Billy said. "You gave away the ending."

The first time I read the Book of Mormon I didn't read as carefully as I should have. All I could think about was the money. But the second time, with Billy, he read so slowly and deliberately that it forced me to pay more attention to the words, especially since I had to help him with some of the bigger ones. Plus, he asked me a lot of questions that made me think about what we were reading. I understood the Book of Mormon much better the second time around.

When we finished our first reading session, we changed into our swimsuits and went outside. Billy yelled and did a cannonball into the pool, soaking me. He showed me how to do the Australian crawl, the back stroke, and the butterfly stroke, while Billy's mom watched us from the kitchen window. When we swam laps, he was much faster than me. It made me wonder which was the more difficult task: teaching Billy how to read like me or teaching me how to swim like him.

CHAPTER 15

The Painting

Over time, Billy made amazing progress in his reading. We spent hours a day reading together. I think the dangling carrot of $50 helped him sit still and concentrate. But he still got frustrated often. It did not come easily to him.

I knew he was improving when I saw him reading the names of the hymns on his own and adding "in the bathroom" to them.

One afternoon while we were reading in 1 Nephi, Billy's dad walked in on us.

"What are you doing?" he asked as I slunk down in a chair.

"We're reading."

"Reading what?"

"The Book of Mormon," Billy said.

Billy's dad snatched the book out of his hands, and with a glint of fury in his eyes, hurled it out the open window.

He glared at me and screamed, "I don't want you reading this garbage in our house!"

"But Mom said I could," Billy said.

"I'm in charge, she's not! I don't want you involved with these Mormons anymore." Then he left the room, slamming the door on his way out.

"It's really not my dad's fault," Billy explained. "He's just mad about his arm, he's mad at me and he's mad about my little brother dying. It's my fault my brother died."

"How was it your fault?" I asked.

"Ever since my brother died, my dad's been mad at me. It must be my fault."

"But that has nothing to do with you," I said. "It's not your fault that your brother died."

Maybe if I grew up thinking I was to blame that my brother died, and maybe if I had a dad who treated me that way, I'd act the same way Billy did at school and at church. I was grateful for my parents.

"I was thinking that if I got baptized," Billy said, "my mom and dad and I could see Ricky again. Maybe my dad could get his arm back. Maybe my dad could like me again."

For the first time, I saw him cry.

"It's not your fault that your brother died," I said again. "I know that if you get baptized and do all the things we're supposed to, we can live forever together with our families."

"I just don't think my dad would ever change," Billy said.

"Does your dad work?"

"No. He used to be a good artist before he lost his arm. But he doesn't paint anymore."

"He's really good," I said.

"He used to do a lot of paintings like that one. He can't now."

We went outside to retrieve the Book of Mormon that Billy's dad had thrown out the window. While we were taping up the ripped pages, I got an idea. After doing all that work to get Billy back to Church and encouraging him to be baptized, now I had to work on Billy's dad. I would definitely need Sister Browning's help, though.

The following Saturday afternoon I stopped by her house. She was in her driveway, washing her Volkswagen Bug.

"It's good to see you Kevin," she said, holding a wet sponge in her hand.

"You know how I'm trying to help Billy?"

"Yes," she said, turning off the hose. "You're doing a wonderful job being a friend to him."

"Well, I think he wants to get baptized now, but his dad won't let him. If you could just talk to Billy's dad, and teach him a lesson like you teach us in Primary, I'm sure he would realize how important it is for Billy to get baptized."

Sister Browning smiled. "Do you think Brother Blankenship would listen to me?"

"Yes."

"Why?"

"Because you are such a great teacher."

"Thanks, Kevin. That's sweet of you to say."

"I just think he needs a friend, like Billy needed a friend," I said. "He's always mad and unhappy. But he's real good at painting. Maybe you could ask him to paint something for you. I bet that would make him happy."

"I think you're right." Then Sister Browning's eyes lit up. "Come with me."

We drove off in her still-wet Volkswagen Bug and arrived at the Blankenship's house.

"What are we doing?" I asked.

"I'm going to try to be a friend to Billy's dad."

After knocking on the door, Billy's mom answered. Sister Browning asked for her husband.

She looked around nervously. "Are you sure you want to talk to him?" she asked.

"I'd like to," Sister Browning said.

"Okay. I'll go get him."

We must have waited on the porch for 10 minutes. I figured he was probably passed out or something.

Finally he came stumbling toward the door.

"Hi, Brother Blankenship," Sister Browning began. "I have a favor to ask of you."

"A favor?"

"Yes. My parents' 30th wedding anniversary is coming up in a couple of months. I've been racking my brain trying to figure out what I could get them. Then I thought about your wonderful paintings. I was wondering if you would be willing to paint a portrait of my parents. It would be a great surprise. I could get you a photo of them. I'd pay you for it, of course."

Billy's dad just looked at her for a moment, as if she had asked him to jump to the moon.

"I haven't painted in a very long time," he said. "It's been years."

"Well, think about it. I'd be honored if you'd do it."

CHAPTER 16

Billy's Birthday Party

Billy turned 12 in June, but he wasn't even close to getting baptized or getting the priesthood. Still, I never forgot to pray for Billy and ask Heavenly Father that he would be able to be baptized.

Billy invited Danny and me to his birthday party—in fact, we were the only ones invited. Billy's mom had told my mom that he had never had a birthday party before because he didn't have any friends to invite before.

For Danny, it was the first time his mom had let him go with us anywhere outside his house or the church.

Billy blew out 12 candles on his cake and opened his presents. I gave Billy a Nerf football and Danny gave him a science kit.

Sister Blankenship gave us a slice of chocolate cake, a bowl of ice cream and glass of milk. Billy drank a gallon of milk all by himself. We never did see Billy's dad. I thought it was strange that he wouldn't even come out for his son's birthday party.

While we were eating ice cream, Sister Browning showed up at the front door. Billy let her in.

"I just came over to wish you a happy birthday," she said to Billy, giving him a hug. Then she handed him a gift. Billy opened the box. Inside was a set of his very own scriptures.

"What do you tell Sister Browning?" Billy's mom said to him.

"Thanks," Billy said.

"You're welcome," Sister Browning replied. "Now you can bring them with you to church."

Sister Blankenship asked Sister Browning if she wanted some cake and ice cream, but Sister Browning said she couldn't stay. "Sorry," she said, "but I've got a date tonight."

I examined Billy's scriptures and saw Sister Browning's inscription on the inside page. Billy let me read it.

Billy,

You are a precious son of our Heavenly Father. He loves you very much. This book teaches us about His love and how we can return to live with Him. I know this book is true. Read it every day and you will be blessed.

Love,

Sister Browning

"You know what I wished for when I blew out my candles?" Billy asked me after I finished reading the inscription.

Before I could tell him that you're not supposed to tell anyone your wish or else it won't come true, he said, "I wished that I could get baptized."

"You should talk to the bishop," I said. "You can be baptized next month!"

"My dad's not going to let me," Billy said. "I just know it. He thinks I need to be older."

I didn't want Billy to wait. What if something happened to him? What if he died while he was waiting to get older and he wasn't able to get baptized?

A couple of days later I went to Sister Browning's house to talk to her about it.

"I was just wondering what happens to a kid that doesn't get baptized when he's eight."

"You mean a Mormon kid?"

"Yeah."

"Well, the scriptures say that if a boy doesn't get baptized when he's eight, the parents will be held accountable," Sister Browning said.

"Does that mean it's the mom and dad's fault if they don't let their kid get baptized?"

"Yes."

"You know how Billy's dad doesn't want him to get baptized? Can't Billy just get baptized without his dad knowing about it? We could sneak him out of the house one day and not tell him. When he gets home and Billy's dad sees that Billy's hair is wet, Billy can just tell him he was swimming."

Sister Browning chuckled. "Would that be honest?"

"No. I guess not. But it's not fair that Billy's dad won't let him get baptized. Can you read Billy's dad that scripture that says it will be his fault if he doesn't let Billy get baptized?"

Sister Browning chuckled again. "No, I don't think that's the right way to go about it. Billy's dad has the right to his opinion and he is Billy's father. We have to respect his wishes. I think Billy needs to talk to his dad about it. If we do our part, then we just need to have faith that Heavenly Father will do His part."

CHAPTER 17

The Slowest Fast Ever

The way I saw things, the clock was ticking on Billy. He had just turned 12 and still wasn't even baptized. Billy was hesitant to talk to his dad about getting baptized and I couldn't blame him. I encouraged him to talk to his dad about it again. The next day, I asked Billy how it went.

"He got mad at me. He told me to quit asking such stupid questions. He said I'm too young and that I need to wait until I'm older."

"How much older?"

"I don't know. My dad probably won't let me get baptized until I'm an old man, like 25. Nothing or nobody will change my dad's mind. My mom has asked him over and over to let me get baptized, but he won't."

"I know someone who could change his mind," I said.

"Who?"

"Heavenly Father."

"How?"

I thought for a moment. "We could fast."

"Fast? What's that?"

"We could pray and tell Heavenly Father that we will go without eating for a whole day."

"What does not eating have to do with getting baptized?"

"When Heavenly Father sees this is something we really want, He will bless us and your dad will *have* to let you get baptized."

"We can't eat *anything?* What about snacks?"

"No. Nothing. Not even a drink."

"Nothing to eat or drink for a whole day? No *milk?* I can't do that. I'd die. Have you ever tried it?"

"Not for a whole day. But I'll do it with you, so you can get baptized."

"Do you think it would work?"

"My mom and dad say it does. Let's try it."

So we set up a day when we could fast. We picked Wednesday because Billy said that his mom usually made meatloaf that night and it wouldn't be as hard to go without as opposed to, say, Friday, which was pizza night.

That morning we ate big breakfasts. I had at least three bowls of cereal. We didn't tell our parents what we were doing because mine had told me we shouldn't go around bragging to people when we're fasting.

At Billy's house, we shut the door of his room. I explained that we needed to start with a prayer and tell Heavenly Father why we were fasting and what blessing we were seeking. We both knelt down by his bed and I told him to say the prayer.

"Why don't you say the prayer?" Billy said.

"But we're fasting for you and your dad," I said. "I think you should do it."

"But I don't know how. I've never prayed before."

Again, I wasn't surprised.

"It's easy," I said. "Start out by saying 'Heavenly Father,' then thank Him for what you have, then tell Him that we're fasting so you can get baptized. You have to end it in the name of Jesus Christ, amen."

"Are you sure He'll listen?"

"Yeah. He will."

"How do you know?"

"One time I had a baseball game and I couldn't find my hat. I looked everywhere. So I knelt down by my bed and said a prayer, asking Heavenly Father to help me find it. When I opened my eyes I saw it on my bed."

"Liar," Billy said.

"No, it's true," I said. "Heavenly Father listens to our prayers. Go ahead and pray. I'll help you if you need it."

Billy knelt in silence for a few minutes before starting. Suddenly he opened his eyes and looked at me. "Can we ask Heavenly Father to help us for more than one thing?" he asked.

"I guess so," I said.

"Well, while we're doing this, then, why don't we ask Heavenly Father to make it so Danny can hear again?"

I wasn't sure about that. Danny's mom had told us that he would never be able to hear. But I didn't want to burst Billy's fragile bubble of faith.

"Okay," I said.

It took Billy a long time to get the words out of his mouth, but when he did, he sounded sincere. He must have felt something. I know I did.

Wouldn't you know it, that afternoon while we were reading the Book of Mormon together and trying hard not to think about food, we could smell cookies baking in the kitchen. Billy's mom soon came into his room with a plateful of chocolate chip cookies and two large glasses of milk.

"Eat up, boys," she said, putting them on Billy's dresser.

"Thanks, Sister Blankenship," I said.

We sat there trying not to look at them—or smell them—while we read.

"My dad says we have to feast upon the word of Christ, which is kind of like feeding our spirits," I told Billy. "When we eat food, we feed our bodies. When we read the scriptures, and fast, we feed our spirits."

"This isn't doing squat for my empty stomach," Billy said.

After 20 minutes, Billy's mom returned to his room to find the cookies and milk untouched.

"What's wrong?" she asked us. "How come you aren't eating?" I tried to think up an excuse, but Billy beat me to it.

"We're going to be swimming in a few minutes," he said. "They say you shouldn't eat before swimming, right? We wouldn't want to get cramps or anything."

Billy's mom gave him a strange look. "Okay," she said. "I'll just keep these in the kitchen until after your swim."

We swam for a while, but neither of us had much energy, so we came inside to continue reading. All those chapters from the writings of Isaiah were confusing. Billy asked me what those things meant and I told him I didn't have a clue. None of it made sense. Things got better when we read about Enos praying all day and all night.

"His knees must have gotten sore," Billy said.

Billy's mom returned. "How about some cookies now?"

"Thanks, mom, but we wouldn't want to spoil our dinner," Billy said.

"Billy, are you feeling all right?" she asked.

"Actually, I'm not," he said. "My stomach hurts a little. I don't feel like eating."

"Me neither," I said.

We were making excuses to avoid eating cookies. Imagine that.

By the time we finished the reading for the day, Billy said, "After all this, my dad *better* let me get baptized."

"Heavenly Father will help us," I said, hoping that He would. I didn't want Billy to lose faith.

For those long 24 hours, my stomach hurt and I was tempted a couple of times to go to the refrigerator and eat something. But I knew I needed to keep my promise to Billy and to Heavenly Father.

The following day, I felt totally weak. I could barely ride my bike to Billy's house. When I arrived, I knocked on the door. Sister Blankenship answered and let me in. "He's in his room," she said. "But he's not feeling very well."

I knew why.

We ended our fast with me offering the prayer. I prayed again that Billy's dad would let Billy get baptized. Then we went to Billy's refrigerator and pantry, grabbing anything that was edible—bread, crackers, apples, pickles—and chowed down as fast as we could like pigs at a trough.

Once we were full, we went on reading the Book of Mormon. Not surprisingly, Billy's favorite part of the book was the violence, like Ammon cutting off arms of the Lamanites trying to steal King Lamoni's sheep. I told him there were a bunch of chapters in Alma about wars, destruction and mayhem, and Billy could hardly contain himself.

The best thing was, after our fast, I actually got Billy to start praying every day before our reading sessions.

Meanwhile, my parents were concerned about me spending so much time with Billy. They thought Billy was headed for you-know-where and that I was going to follow him all the way there. I wanted to tell them about all of the progress Billy was making, but I decided not to.

I didn't think they would believe it. I could hardly believe it myself.

CHAPTER 18

Boys of Summer

As a kid, I loved summer days. No school, no homework, just long hours frolicking in the warm sun. When we weren't reading the Book of Mormon, Billy and I were determined to wring every last drop of fun we could out of each day.

Billy and I signed up to play little league baseball and we wanted Danny to play with us, too, though he had never played before. We had asked if Danny could play, but his parents said no. I don't think they wanted him to play any sports. Too dangerous, they said. Maybe when he gets older, they said.

So in the spring we went to his house and taught him everything we knew about baseball. One time, Billy threw the ball and it hit Danny right in the head, giving him a black eye. Billy felt bad. It took a couple of weeks before Danny's mom would let us play baseball again at his house. When she did, Billy was more careful. He was so patient with him, helping him to catch and hit. Meanwhile, we got pretty good at sign language and at one point, we hardly even noticed anymore that he was deaf.

After constantly asking Danny's parents if he could play baseball, they relented when they found out that Brother Woodson was going to be our coach.

It was kind of hard to remember to call him "Coach Woodson" instead of "Brother Woodson" and I slipped sometimes. It turned out that Brother Woodson was a huge baseball fan. He had season tickets to the Dodgers and he took us a couple of times.

He taught us a lot about baseball and about the gospel, and he liked to tell us analogies that applied to both. When he'd drive Billy and me home after practices, he'd share them with us.

"Baseball is a microcosm of life. In baseball, the goal is to score runs and to get back to where we started from—home plate. But there are obstacles in our way—the pitcher and the fielders. We have to use everything we have, our eyes, our feet, our arms, our legs, and our heads to make our way around the bases. Luckily, we have those bases to keep us safe. We have coaches at first and third bases, guiding us. In life, it's the same thing. We're trying to return home—a heavenly home. To get there, we have a lot of things to overcome. We need to try our best, and use the 'bases' the Lord has given us, like church, the priesthood, and the commandments, so we can be safe. We need to listen to our leaders, who guide us. If we do, we can make it back to our heavenly home."

I don't know how much of the gospel-related stuff sunk in for Billy.

"Did you know the best hitters in Major League Baseball fail 70 percent of the time?" Brother Woodson asked us.

"What do you mean?" Billy asked.

"What I mean is, great hitters like Rod Carew and George Brett and Pete Rose fail to get on base seven out of ten trips to the plate. If they are safe three times out of ten—or what we call hitting .300—they are doing really well."

"So?"

"So being a good baseball player, and being successful in life, is all about trying even after we fail. If we make a mistake, we can repent and try again. We can't ever give up. The Lord will never give up on us. So we shouldn't ever give up on ourselves."

Once, Billy dropped a fly ball and let out a string of expletives and slammed his glove to the ground. I was glad Danny couldn't hear him. I wished I hadn't.

Coach Woodson immediately marched toward Billy and in a stern but loving voice, said, "Billy, this team has some rules. One of those rules is 'no swearing.' I want you to run five laps around the park."

"Five laps?" Billy protested. "That's a stupid rule. My dad and I swear all the time at my house. That rule has nothing to do with baseball."

"Well, if your dad lets you swear at home, that's his business," Coach Woodson replied. "But on my team, we don't use that kind of language."

"I don't want to play on your team anymore," Billy said, stomping toward the bench. "I don't want to play for a coach with stupid rules."

Billy sulked the rest of practice.

Afterwards, Coach Woodson pulled Billy and me aside. He shook his head and smiled.

"Billy, I don't know whether to slug you or hug you," he said. "If you don't want to play with us anymore, that's up to you. If you want to play on a different team, you can. I hope you stay with us, because I like you. But on my team we don't talk like that. Someday you're going to be a priesthood holder. Priesthood holders don't use that kind of language."

Billy kicked the dirt with his cleats. Then he took off running. For a while, I didn't know if he was running home or running laps. As it turned out, he ran those five laps and returned, out of breath.

He didn't utter another swear word the rest of the season.

Our team, the Giants, was pretty good, and Billy was the star. He batted third in the lineup and played shortstop, third base and pitcher. Billy would collect two or three hits in every game—he even smacked five home runs that season. He could hit the ball hard and one time he knocked a third baseman's glove clean off the player's hand on a line drive. Every time he came to bat, kids in the outfield would back up near the fence.

Once I asked Billy his secret to hitting the ball so hard. "It's easy," he said. "I just pretend the ball is the head of someone I don't like."

Hey, whatever works, I guess.

Billy made some amazing plays in the field. He had an uncanny knack for catching the ball, as if he had some sort of magnet inside his glove. I mostly played second base and watched in awe as Billy caught any ball hit within the same zip code. He was lightning fast around the bases and had a howitzer for an arm.

Danny, on the other hand, batted last in the lineup and was relegated to right field, where he could do the least amount of damage. He spent most of our games picking dandelions. He could barely catch a baseball. When a fly ball came his way, he'd cower and cover his head. A couple of times, he got hit square on the crown of his cranium with a ball.

At the plate, it was worse. Coach Woodson called out instructions to him from the third base coach's box, trying to correct his stance.

"Scoot toward the plate," Coach Woodson yelled in vain. From the bleachers, Danny's dad would sign to Danny to move closer and he'd inch slightly inside the batter's box. His dad would urge him to swing with hand movements but poor Danny would usually swing right after the ball settled into the catcher's glove. Other kids would laugh and deride Danny pretty hard. But when they did, Billy got angry.

After one of Danny's inglorious strikeouts, the catcher on the other team pointed at Danny and made a joke.

Billy saw and heard it, and I saw him glare at the catcher, clench his teeth and make a fist with his right hand.

The next time Billy came to the plate, he belted a line drive into the gap in left-center, one of those balls that rolled all the way to the fence. At first, I thought Billy would stretch that into a stand-up triple, easily, if not score a home run.

But Billy slowed up while rounding second.

"What are you doing?!" Coach Woodson screamed from the coach's box. "Run, Billy!"

Nobody could believe it when Billy started trotting toward third. Just then, he saw the relay throw coming toward the second baseman and Billy sped up again, passing third base. As the second baseman hurled the ball toward home, I could see what Billy was up to. Just as the catcher snagged the ball, Billy plowed him over, jarring the ball loose and knocking the catcher to the ground. As the catcher lay writhing in pain, Billy pumped his fists.

The opposing coach was livid, but the umpire let the play stand.

After the game, Coach Woodson took the team to get some ice cream. "Didn't I look like Pete Rose on that play at the plate?" Billy asked us just before he inhaled a giant bite of triple hot fudge sundae.

"Billy, you know what you did was wrong," Coach Woodson said.

"That kid deserved it," Billy said. "He made fun of Danny. Plus, it scored us a run!"

"Well, you didn't score you any runs in heaven today. You really hurt that catcher badly. You may have broken his jaw and wrist. You can't go around hurting people who hurt you. That can get you in a lot of trouble. That's why I'm suspending you from our next game."

"What's suspending?" Billy asked.

"It means I'm not allowing you to play."

"That's not fair!"

"You injured that boy intentionally and he won't play the rest of the season. Doesn't that make you feel bad?"

"How are we going to win if I can't play?"

"There are more important things in life than winning games," Coach Woodson said.

"Like what?"

"Like following Jesus Christ and being like Him. When you get baptized and receive the priesthood, you will promise to do that. You can't change what's happened. So what do you think the Lord would want you to do now?"

Billy stared glumly into his empty bowl of ice cream.

A couple of days later, with Coach Woodson's help, Billy found out the catcher's name and address. They showed up at his house with a gallon of ice cream. Billy apologized for what he had done.

Later, I asked him about it.

"He's nicer than he looks," Billy said of the catcher. "When I left, I had a good feeling. It was weird."

I think he meant a good kind of weird. While I didn't agree with the way Billy went about it, I was impressed by the way he stuck up for Danny.

All in all, it was a great baseball season. For the first time in my little league career I was on a team with a winning record. Not only that, but we advanced to the league championship.

Going into the final game against the Yankees, Danny hadn't gotten a hit all year. In fact, he hadn't even scored. He got on base twice all season, on walks, but one of those times he was so excited he forgot to tag up on a fly ball and created a double play situation for the other team. While he sat on the bench and cried, Billy put his arm around him and told him he would make up for it the next inning. Sure enough, Billy crushed a home run over the centerfield wall and we won the game. We had a record of 10-2. One of those games we lost was when Billy was serving his suspension. The Yankees beat us that day 17-1.

When we beat the Reds and advanced to the championship

game against those same Yankees, we were a little worried about the way they had manhandled us. On the other hand, we knew we would have Billy this time and we were out to avenge that loss.

Before the game started, I could tell Billy was acting differently. When I looked in the bleachers and saw his dad show up for the first time, I figured out why. I also saw Sister Browning in the crowd. That made me extra nervous.

Billy's dad sat by my parents and Danny's parents. He fidgeted while they tried making small talk with him.

Since Billy had pitched three innings against the Reds, Coach Woodson had Casey start out at pitcher. He was knocked around pretty good. After three innings, the Yankees were up 8-3 and acting like they had already won the championship.

Going into the fourth inning, Coach Woodson asked Billy if he was okay to pitch the rest of the game. Billy said he was.

Turned out, Billy was more than okay, mowing down one Yankee batter after another. He pitched the final three innings, which included seven strikeouts and zero walks. For most of the game, I noticed Billy's dad sitting there with a stoic look on his face, as if he were sitting in a museum. Gradually he started to get into the game and by the time Billy had struck out the last batter in the top of the sixth inning, Billy's dad was standing and smiling.

As we went into that final at-bat of the season, down 8-6, Coach Woodson gathered us around him.

"I want you to know that I'm proud of you guys," he said. "Your parents are proud of you, too. You've worked really hard this season. I just want you to have fun and enjoy our last inning together. No matter what happens, it's been a terrific season."

Then he paused and a grin spread across his face.

"But I'd really like to win this game."

"Go Giants!" we all yelled.

When Coach Woodson looked at the lineup card posted in the dugout to see who was batting, his smile disappeared. We were at the bottom of the order, beginning with me. "Kevin, John and Danny," he said with as much conviction his voice could muster under the circumstances. "Everybody be a hitter!"

My nerves were frazzled as I placed my helmet on my head and walked to the on-deck circle. I didn't want to make the first out and let my team down.

Before I took a practice swing, Billy approached me and slapped my helmet.

"C'mon, Kevin," he said. "Get on base."

If we had any chance of winning, I knew that we needed to get Billy to the plate one last time. When I stepped into the batter's box, I exhaled and peered out to the mound, where a kid who was twice my size was standing. I swear he had a mustache.

On the first pitch, I took a mighty cut and fouled it off to the backstop. Then I took a pitch high for a ball.

"Look for your pitch, Kevin," Coach Woodson said.

I swung and missed on the next offering. I could feel my whole body tightening up, knowing one more strike would give us our first out. The next pitch came hurtling toward me and I backed up a bit. But the ball broke inside and painted the inside corner of the plate. Strike three. The umpire called me out, and as I returned to the dugout, the Yankees went berserk.

"I'm sorry," I told Coach Woodson.

"It's okay, Kevin," he said. "That was a tough pitch to handle."

After that, John grounded out to the shortstop. Suddenly we were down to our final out. It was all up to Danny, who hadn't gotten a hit, or scored a run, all season. The sense on both sides was that the game was over.

"Easy out!" the Yankee fielders were chattering.

I prayed with all my heart for Danny, that somehow he could

draw a walk and get on base to extend the season for at least one more batter. If only he could get on base on a walk, I thought, we would be back at the top of the order.

It was funny, though. Despite the pressure of the situation, Danny, instead of looking nervous, wore an expression of dogged determination. On the first two pitches, Danny swung and missed badly. We were down to our final strike. I was thinking about what I might say to console Danny when he struck out.

Suddenly, Billy walked out of the dugout. "Umpire, time out," he said.

The umpire looked at him strangely, then granted the request.

"Billy," Coach Woodson said, "I'm the one who's supposed to call time out. What are you doing?"

"I need to tell Danny something."

So Billy and Danny conferred in the on-deck circle, with Billy doing some sort of sign language. Then he came back to the dugout with a smile.

"What did you tell him?" I asked.

"You'll see," he responded.

I watched Danny move toward the back of the batter's box and turn his feet slightly toward third base. As the Yankee pitcher went into his windup, everything seemed to go in slow motion. The pitch came toward Danny. He swung—and connected. The ball rolled between the second and first baseman and reached the grass in shallow right field.

Danny was so excited to make contact that he almost forgot to run to first base. The rightfielder ran up on the ground ball and whipped it to the first baseman. Danny barely made it safely. Our dugout, and our fans, erupted.

It wasn't just that Danny had kept our season alive, but it was that Danny had overcome an obstacle of Goliath-like proportions. Just seeing his 100-watt smile as he stood on first base, getting his first hit in his final at-bat, almost made me cry.

That brought up the top of the order. The Yankees pitcher must have been flustered after Danny had gotten a hit off of him, because he walked our next two batters to load the bases. Danny stood at third, waiting for Billy to bring him home.

Billy worked the count full before driving a fastball deep into left-center field. Danny and our two other baserunners crossed the plate, giving us a dramatic 9-8 win—and the league championship.

Though Billy earned the game-winning hit, everyone mobbed Danny. He was the real hero for coming through when all the pressure in the world was on him.

It was a great way to finish the season. What topped it all off, though, was when I saw Billy's dad hug Billy with his one arm during our celebration.

Billy went on to make the league All-Star team. When a game was scheduled for Sunday, Billy said he wouldn't play.

"I've got church that day," he told the All-Star coach.

When I heard that, I figured all those lessons Brother Woodson taught us that summer had penetrated Billy's thick skull.

CHAPTER 19

The Rescue

After our daily Book of Mormon reading, Billy and I had swimming races in his pool, seeing who could be the first to swim 10 laps. Billy always beat me by four or five laps.

Billy said it was time to go somewhere else and try out my swimming skills.

"Where?" I asked.

"The beach."

"I'm not allowed to go there by myself."

"You won't be by yourself," he said. "I'll be there, too. Don't worry. Nothing's going to happen."

Billy said he wanted to invite Danny. He called his mom.

"I'm sorry, but Danny's not allowed to go to the beach," she said. That's what my mom would have said, too.

Billy had a boogie board and he said it would be fun to try it. So we rode our bikes to the beach.

We arrived and I decided to just soak my feet for a minute and get out.

Billy, of course, had no fear of the water or the waves. I just kept thinking about the time the undertow got me when I was six and I didn't want it to happen again.

"Get in!" Billy shouted. "The water's warm. When I get baptized, this is where I want to do it. Will they let you get baptized in the ocean?"

"I don't think so," I said. "There's a baptismal font in the church. That's where they do the baptisms."

"Oh," Billy said. "This is where I want to be baptized. Wasn't Jesus baptized in the ocean?"

"Actually, it was a river," I said.

I waded out slowly and carefully as I watched Billy get on his boogie board and paddle far out into the ocean. When big waves came, he rode the boogie board to the shore.

"C'mon, Kevin," he said as he reached the sand. "Don't be a chicken. Just hold on to the boogie board. It will keep you above the water. Besides, you know how to swim good now. I taught you."

True, but I still wasn't comfortable swimming in the ocean. But I decided to get on Billy's boogie board. When I got chest-deep in the water, I started shuddering violently. Part of it was because the water was cold. Mostly, I was scared.

"Lay down on the board!" Billy shouted at me from the safety of the shoreline.

I did as he told me and I began paddling out further into the water. I bobbed up and down with the waves until I saw a large wave heading right for me. I gripped the board as hard as I could and started paddling for shore. The wave rumbled louder and louder as it approached, like an oncoming train, and I just wanted to get out of there. Suddenly I felt myself being picked up by the force of the water. My body tilted and flipped over. Before I knew it, I was under the board, under the water, and struggling for air. Salt water filled my head, burning my nose. I had felt that sensation before and couldn't believe I had put myself in that position again. My arms and legs flew around frantically and I was certain I was going to die this time. It seemed the harder I fought to find my way to the surface, the more I stayed under the water. It was like I was paralyzed. Panicked, I had forgotten everything that Billy had taught me about swimming.

As I tumbled like a sock in a clothes dryer, I thought of how disappointed my parents would be in me for disobeying them.

In my mind, I prayed like I had never prayed before. I begged Heavenly Father to save me. Then I felt something, or someone, grab me by the arm and drag me to the sand. I looked up and saw Billy.

"Kevin, are you okay?" he asked.

I responded by coughing and throwing up a pint of water. I lay on the beach for quite a while. I was grateful to be alive.

Part of me was mad that Billy had pressured me into the ocean. At the same time, I was glad Billy had rescued me. Before we went home, I thanked Billy for saving my life. He was a hero, but I didn't tell anyone about what had happened.

CHAPTER 20

The Surprise Visitor

That summer, to everyone's shock, Billy's dad showed up at church for the first time in years.

He wore faded Levis, a multi-colored tank top and blue flip-flops. His stump was covered with a red bandana and his hair was tied back in a ponytail. His mere presence created quite a stir, and people went out of their way to greet him. Throughout the chapel, people whispered to one another, "Why is he here?"

Billy's dad looked uncomfortable. But I could tell Billy was happy to have his dad at church. I barely recognized Billy. For the occasion, his hair was combed nicely and it looked like his mom had bought him some new clothes—ones that fit and didn't have holes or stains.

Billy's dad came into our Primary class.

"Sister Browning?" he said.

"Brother Blankenship, it's very nice to see you."

"I need to talk to you afterwards," he said, then sat down in one of the chairs.

"I'd be happy to," she said.

Sister Browning started her lesson by saying, "We'd like to welcome Brother Blankenship, um, Billy's dad, to class."

It just so happened that the lesson that day was on baptism. Knowing Sister Browning, she probably changed the lesson at the last minute.

"Who can tell us what baptism is?" Sister Browning asked.

"It's a promise between us and Heavenly Father," I said.

"That's right, Kevin. Let's get out our scriptures and read Mosiah 18:8-10 to learn more about what this baptismal covenant is."

Of course, Skyler found it right away. "Do I get a prize for being first?" he asked Sister Browning.

"This isn't a race, Skyler," she said. "I'm sure if scripture chasing ever becomes an Olympic event, you'd win a gold medal."

After I found the scripture reference, I helped Billy find it in his new scriptures, too. I looked over at Billy's dad. His eyes were closed and I wondered if he was asleep.

"In these verses, Alma is teaching the people about baptism at a place called the waters of Mormon," Sister Browning said.

"Is that where the Mormons back then went swimming?" Billy asked.

"Sort of," Sister Browning said. "Who'd like to read the scripture?"

To everyone's surprise, Billy raised his hand.

"Okay, Billy," Sister Browning said. And Billy began reading slowly and carefully:

"*And it came to pass that he said unto them: Behold, here are the waters of Mormon (for thus were they called) and now, as ye are desirous to come into the fold of God, and to be called his people, and are willing to bear one another's burdens, that they may be light;*

"*Yea, and are willing to mourn with those that mourn; yea and comfort those that stand in need of comfort, and to stand as witnesses of God at all times and in all things, and in all places that ye may be in, even until death, that ye may be redeemed of God, and be numbered with those of the first resurrection, that ye may have eternal life—*

"*Now I say unto you, if this be the desire of your hearts, what have you against being baptized in the name of the Lord, as a witness before him that ye have entered into a covenant with him, that ye will serve him and keep his commandments, that he may pour out his Spirit more abundantly upon you?"*

When Billy finished reading, I was relieved. It took him a while to read the passage and he butchered a few words, but I realized my reading sessions with Billy were paying off. It was the first time Sister Browning had ever heard him read. I was proud of Billy. I think Billy's dad was proud of him, too.

"Thank you, Billy," Sister Browning said. "You did a very good job. Let's break it up into pieces and see if we can figure out what Alma is telling the people, and us, about baptism. What does 'desirous to come into the fold of God and be called his people' mean?"

"That we want to follow Jesus?" I said.

"That's right, Kevin. When we are baptized, we become members of Jesus' church, or the Church of Jesus Christ of Latter-day Saints. We take upon ourselves His name. Billy, tell me your last name."

"You already know my last name," Billy said.

"I know, but tell me anyway."

"Blankenship."

"Why is that your last name?"

Billy looked over at his dad. "Because it's my dad's last name."

"That's right. Because you are his son, and because you love your dad, you've taken upon yourself his name. When we are baptized, who's name do we take upon ourselves?"

"Jesus Christ's," said Skyler.

"So when you get baptized, you have to change your last name?" Billy asked.

"No, not literally," Sister Browning replied. "But we agree to live our lives like Jesus did, as if His name was part of our names. Next, it says, 'are willing to bear one another's burdens, that they may be light. Yea, and are willing to mourn with those that mourn.' What does 'mourn' mean?"

"Like waking up early in the morn?" Billy said.

I could tell Skyler wanted to ridicule Billy for his answer, but he didn't—probably because Billy's dad was in the room.

"It means to be sad," Skyler said, rolling his eyes.

"Have any of you been really sad about something?" Sister Browning asked.

"When my little brother died, my mom and dad were really sad," Billy said. "If Jesus has the power to do these miracles and stuff, why do you think He let my brother die?"

"We don't know why things like that happen," Sister Browning said. "But Jesus promised us that if we keep His commandments that we can see those who died again and live with them forever."

"Did you hear that?" Billy exclaimed, turning to his dad. "We can see Ricky again someday!"

I looked and saw tears streaming down Billy's dad's cheeks. It got awfully quiet in that classroom.

"That's one of the promises Heavenly Father makes with us when we're baptized," said Sister Browning. "If we are willing to stand up for what's right, even when it's not easy, throughout our lives, He promises us eternal life. That means we can be resurrected and live forever with Heavenly Father, Jesus and our families."

"What is resurrected?" Billy asked.

"Three days after Jesus died, He came alive again," Sister Browning said. "His body and His spirit came together. We will all be resurrected, too, someday. And we'll never die again. Our bodies will be changed and become perfect."

"You mean like *The Six Million Dollar Man*?" Billy said.

"Kind of."

"*Steve Austin: astronaut*," Billy intoned, perfectly imitating the opening of *The Six Million Dollar Man*. "*A man barely alive. We can rebuild him. We have the technology. We can make him better than he was. Better . . . stronger . . . faster.*"

"Something like that," Sister Browning said.

"You mean my dad will have his arm back and Danny will be able to hear when they are resurrected?" Billy said.

"Yes," Sister Browning said.

"That's cool," Billy said. "But why can't we wait until we're older to be baptized?"

"Yeah," Skyler said. "Why do we get baptized when we're eight instead of 30, when Jesus was baptized?"

"Those are great questions. Heavenly Father said that we should be baptized when we're eight," Sister Browning replied. "That's what's called the 'age of accountability.' At eight, we are accountable, or responsible, for the things we do. And like I said, when we are baptized we receive the gift of the Holy Ghost, which can help us throughout our lives. Wouldn't you want that gift your whole life?"

"If I get baptized, won't it mean I can't have any fun?" Billy asked.

"Heavenly Father wants us to be happy," Sister Browning said. "We can have fun and still obey the commandments. The reason He gave us the commandments is to help us be happy."

"Wouldn't it be better if we got baptized when we're really old, just before we die?" Billy asked. "That way, we can do whatever we want. What's the point of being baptized, having your sins washed away, only to keep on sinning the next day? And the day after that?"

"What if I told you to walk through a long, dark cave by yourself?" Sister Browning said. "What do you think would happen?"

"I'd probably get lost," I said.

"That's right. Now what if I told you to walk through a long, dark cave by yourself, but with a flashlight?"

"It would make it a lot easier," Billy said.

"Exactly. After your baptism, you receive the gift of the Holy Ghost, which is like that flashlight. It can help you avoid mistakes and getting lost. As long as we keep that flashlight on by choosing the right, we won't get lost in life. When we do make mistakes, we can repent and be forgiven. That's why it's important to take the sacrament every week so we can renew our covenants we made at baptism."

Sister Browning had a way of explaining things so they were easy to understand.

"Well, our time's about up," Sister Browning said. "I want to tell you that I know the things we talked about today, about baptism, are true. When we are baptized, we promise to follow Jesus during our lives and Jesus promises to bless us during our lives and even after this life."

Sister Browning asked who would like to offer the closing prayer. Billy raised his hand, which surprised everybody.

"Thank you, Billy," Sister Browning said.

Billy bowed his head and closed his eyes. "Heavenly Father, thanks for the things Sister Browning taught us. Thanks for bringing my dad to church. Please tell him to let me get baptized so I can see my little brother again. In the name of Jesus Christ, amen."

The kids in class kind of looked at Billy, as if wondering, "What happened to the Billy Blankenship we loved to hate?" It was like a Billy was transforming right before our eyes.

When we got up to leave, Sister Browning opened a large sack. "We were talking about gifts earlier and there's a gift I would like to give to each of you," she said.

Inside were a bunch of square packages wrapped in brightly colored paper. She handed each of us a present with our name on it and asked us to open them. We each received the same gift —our very own journal.

"Skyler will be leaving our class when he receives the priesthood in a couple of weeks. I hope that each of you will write about your experiences as you receive the priesthood. You can write every day about everything that's happening in your lives."

Everyone left the classroom except for Sister Browning, Billy's dad, Billy and me.

"I've been thinking about your offer to do that painting of your folks," Billy's dad said. "That's why I came here today. I appreciate it, but I wanted to tell you that I can't paint your picture for you."

"Do you mind me asking why?"

"Before my accident, I was an artist. I'm not an artist anymore. I haven't done any painting since then. I'm not left-handed."

"That may be true," Sister Browning said, "but I've seen your work and I was very impressed. Heavenly Father has blessed you with a real talent. I think your artistic talent is still inside you. It comes from your heart and your mind. I'm sure if you try, your left hand can learn what your right hand used to do."

Billy's dad struggled for a response. "It wouldn't be as good as I could have done before Vietnam," he said.

"That's okay. I believe in you."

"Are you sure you want me to do it?"

"Absolutely," Sister Browning said.

"I guess I could give it a try," he finally said.

"So how much would you charge to do a portrait of my parents from a photo?"

"Well, I, uh . . ."

"How about two hundred dollars?"

"Two hundred dollars?"

That sounded like a lot of money to me.

"Is that not enough?"

"No, that's enough. Thank you."

"Okay," Sister Browning said. "My parents' anniversary is in one month. Does that give you enough time?"

"I'll do my best."

"Great," Sister Browning said. "I'll drop off the photo tomorrow."

CHAPTER 21

(Un)answered Prayers

During one of our reading and swimming sessions, Billy showed me how he was writing in his journal.

"Have you written in your journal?" he asked me.

"No, not yet."

"Look at mine," he said.

He had drawn some pictures and some words.

"This is my brother," he said, showing me a stick figure. "I can't wait to see him again. I've written 27 pages so far. I've been writing every day." His handwriting looked like chicken scratch—I could barely read it—but it seemed to be therapeutic for him to get all of his feelings down on paper like that.

"Twenty-seven pages?" I said. "That's a lot. I couldn't think up that much to write. Nothing interesting ever happens to me. What do you write about?"

"About my brother and all the things we'll do together when I see him again," Billy said. "But I can't be good all the time, like you. I can't even read. I'm not smart."

"You're smart," I said. "You just need to keep practicing reading. The Lord is helping you. When you get baptized, you start over. It's like you become a brand new person. Remember when we were playing kick ball at recess a few months ago and you kicked the ball into the bushes?"

"Yeah," Billy said. "I got a do-over."

"Yeah!" I said. "A do-over. That's what baptism is like, getting a do-over. We promise Heavenly Father and Jesus that from now on we're going to do better. They help us do better."

Unfortunately, summer ended and we had to go back to school. Billy and I started sixth grade. Again we were in the same class. With all the reading Billy had done over the summer, he did much better in his schoolwork.

One day, Billy said he wanted to talk to me during recess. We walked to the end of the grass field where we could be alone and no one else could hear us. We sat down against the fence.

"How long does it take for a prayer to be answered?" Billy asked me.

"What do you mean?" I asked.

"You know how I've been praying that my dad would let me get baptized?"

"Yeah."

"When do you think Heavenly Father will answer my prayer?"

"I don't know," I said. "I think He's already answering that prayer."

"How?"

"Well, your dad went to church, didn't he?"

"Yeah, I guess. You said only Heavenly Father could make him go to church and he did. But we stopped eating for a whole day and my dad still won't let me get baptized. Why?"

"My mom says that we have to be patient."

"Well, I don't have time for that."

"Have you said anything to your dad about getting baptized since he went to church?"

"I asked him again if I could get baptized and he told me the same thing, that I was too young."

"My mom and dad say that Heavenly Father answers all prayers, but not always the way we want them."

"What do you mean?"

"A couple of years ago, when I was little, I prayed that I would get a pet turtle for Christmas. Instead, I got Lincoln Logs."

"That stinks."

"Yeah. I told my mom and dad and they said Heavenly Father knows what's best for us and that we don't always know what's best for us. I still can't understand why Lincoln Logs were better for me than a turtle, though."

"Do you think Heavenly Father wants me to get baptized?"

"Of course. He wants everyone to get baptized."

There was a pause.

"Is your dad doing that painting for Sister Browning?" I asked.

"I think so. He won't let me see it. But he seems happy being able to do something he likes to do. It keeps him busy. He hasn't been drinking and he doesn't yell at me as much as he used to."

We continued talking, but I noticed it was awfully quiet. I looked around and the playground was deserted. I gulped.

"We missed the bell!" I shouted. Then I jumped to my feet and ran as fast as I could to the school. Billy didn't act concerned, but he ran with me anyway.

When I got to my class, Mrs. Perkins told us to go to the principal's office and they called my mom because I was so late.

"What were you and Billy doing together for 20 minutes after the bell had rung?" Mom asked.

"Just talking," I said. "I'm really sorry. It won't happen again."

"You bet it won't. You're grounded for three days. No friends, no TV. Do you understand me?"

"Yes, Mom."

CHAPTER 22

Testimony Meeting

During our swimming sessions together I noticed I was getting faster. I have to say that Billy was a pretty good teacher. He was patient with me, just like I was patient with him on his reading.

I continued spending a lot of time at Billy's house and Billy's dad acted nicer toward me. He even said hi to me a few times. Billy's dad didn't seem to mind that we were reading the Book of Mormon anymore, either. I wondered how a grown man who had been baptized could stop going to church and forget the promises he made to Heavenly Father.

I didn't see him much, though I knew he was there. Billy told me that his dad converted a room of the house into an art studio and that he was probably working on that painting that Sister Browning had commissioned him to do.

Anyway, Billy and I continued praying every day that his dad would give Billy permission to be baptized. After that appearance in our Primary class, Billy's dad started coming to church on a regular basis. He'd just sit in the back, trying to be inconspicuous, but when you have hair cascading to your waist, only one arm, and you wear faded Levis and a T-shirt to church, it's hard to be inconspicuous.

Meanwhile, I started paying more attention to the deacons passing the sacrament on Sundays. I wanted to be like them. Skyler had just been ordained a deacon and I watched him closely.

I watched all of them—what they wore, how they acted, what they did. So did Billy. He'd ask me all sorts of questions about the sacrament and he said he would like to do it someday.

It was Fast Sunday, and after the sacrament, the bishop excused the deacons to sit with their families, then he bore his testimony. My mind was wandering that day, as it usually did on fast Sunday. I was thinking about the roast beef and potatoes that were cooking in the oven at home and I tortured myself by imagining the pleasant aromas that would greet me when I walked through the door.

After the bishop sat down, Brother Eichorn stood to bear his testimony. He had Alzheimer's, so he said the same thing every month, retelling stories about his youth. It was kind of like watching a rerun on TV. Everyone knew exactly what he was going to say before he said it.

Sister Goodrich stood and talked about how difficult it had been for her husband to be out of work. She thanked the ward for its concern and generosity during that time of great distress.

Things were going pretty routinely, until out of the corner of my eye I saw Billy's dad making his way to the stand. On that day he wore a lime green leisure suit, a neon orange tie and blue flip-flops. Everyone braced for what was to come.

He looked so frightened up there. Come to think of it, so did Bishop Sweeten. Billy's dad must have stood there for a minute or so, just staring into the audience. My family and I were sitting on the fifth row, as we usually did, and we had a good view of Brother Blankenship. I noticed tears dripping down his cheeks.

Finally, he cleared his throat. "Forgive me," he began. For many of the people in the ward, those were the first words they had ever heard him speak. "It's been a long time since I've done this," he said.

Like most people in the ward, I was surprised to hear that he had spoken in church before.

"Most of you don't know me. My name is Eddie Blankenship. I'd like to tell you a little bit about myself. I'm originally from Oregon. I grew up in a great family. My dad was a bishop for many years and my brothers and sisters and I always had fun together. We went to church every Sunday. We had Family Home Evening every Monday.

"My mom was an angel of a woman. She taught me how to pray. She taught me to read by reading the Book of Mormon. She loved us kids so much. But when I got to high school, I started to run around with friends who liked to do things my parents had taught me not to do. I resisted for a while. But my friends made their arguments about why it was okay. 'Are you going to let your parents or some old men of some church tell you how to run your life? You're missing out on so many things!' Over time, I gradually began doing those things they were doing.

"Not long after I graduated from high school, I got married to a girl from my ward. They didn't say it, but I'm sure my parents were heartbroken when I decided not to go on a mission. My wife and I left for college. My dream was to become an artist. I've always been good at drawing and painting. But my plans changed during my sophomore year, when I was drafted into the military and sent to boot camp. The night before I left, my dad gave me a blessing. I remember him placing his hands on my head and promising me that I would be kept safe from harm if I would keep the commandments.

"After the blessing, I hugged my dad and resolved in my heart that I would. A few months later, I was sent to Vietnam at a time when the fighting was at its worst. I won't tell you the atrocities that I saw there, but every once in a while, I still wake up in a cold sweat, reliving those awful moments of death and destruction. I was the only Mormon in my platoon and I was embarrassed to go to church or pray. After a while, I started doing what the other guys were doing. They justified it and it sounded okay in my mind. I was thousands of miles away from home, in a strange land. There were things I felt I needed to do to survive. In my spare time, I'd take out my notepad and draw pictures of things I saw in Vietnam."

Billy's dad paused, trying to control his emotions before continuing.

"One night, we were out on patrol when we started taking enemy fire. Three guys in my platoon died before my eyes. I wondered if the same would happen to me. A week later, I saw a beautiful wood carving lying on the ground near our camp. I thought it would be a great souvenir to bring home. I remember bending down, picking it up and hearing a deafening explosion. The next thing I remembered was waking up in a hospital bed. A doctor explained to me that he had to amputate my right arm and said I was lucky I didn't lose my leg, too. That carving had been booby-trapped by the enemy. My dreams of becoming an artist were over.

"I remembered my father's blessing. I had not been obedient. As I lay in that hospital bed, recovering, all I could think about was how unfair life was. I doubted that there was a God. Even if there were a God, I decided, there was no way to repent. It was too late. There was no way I could be forgiven.

"Not long after I returned from Vietnam, my parents died in a car accident. Then, several years ago, before we moved to this area, our baby, Ricky, died. At that point, I shut God out of my life completely. Until recently.

"My son, Billy, is the reason I'm here today. He is trying to be a good boy. He's been asking me lately if he could get baptized and join the Church. I've been telling him no. But I've watched him saying his prayers and reading the scriptures. It's reminded me of a peaceful, happy time in my life, when I was a kid. I feel like it's like my parents' way of telling me it's time to return to the Church. I went to Billy's Primary class a few weeks ago and while I was sitting back there in my seat, I felt something I hadn't felt in many years. I can't explain my feelings, other than to say for the first time in a long time, I felt peace. I want those feelings all the time. I know those feelings come from the Lord Jesus. I've been meeting with Bishop Sweeten lately and he's helped me to understand that, through the Savior, forgiveness is possible. There is a way back.

"I want Billy to know that I know, deep down, that the gospel is true. I don't want him to go through all the suffering I've gone through in my life. I want Billy to know that I've decided to let him get baptized. And, when he's ready, he can receive the Aaronic Priesthood."

At that moment, I felt as light as a feather, as though I was going to lift right out of my seat. I was so happy for Billy. When I looked over at him, he was beaming. I was so happy that Heavenly Father had answered our many prayers.

"I want to be the kind of father Billy deserves and the kind of husband my dear wife deserves. I appreciate you listening to me. Thank you for being accepting of me and my family. I'm sorry for the times I may have offended you. I'm asking for your help as I try to come back to the Church."

Billy's dad seemed like a different person than the one who cursed Billy and me out at his house a few months earlier.

When I talked to Billy after church, I congratulated him. "Who's going to baptize you?" I asked.

"I don't know."

"Bishop Sweeten could," I suggested.

"I guess that would be okay. I like him."

Then I got a brilliant idea.

"Why don't you ask your dad if he can baptize you?"

"Can he?"

"He can if he holds the priesthood."

A few days later, Billy and I walked into the living room of his house and sat next to his dad.

"Dad, thanks again for letting me get baptized," he said.

"If you're going to do it, that means you're going to go to church every Sunday and do the things you're asked to," his dad said.

"I will. I was just wondering if you could baptize me."

Billy's dad looked at his son and trembled.

"I can't, son," he said, tears falling from his eyes.

"But you have the priesthood, right? Maybe you could talk to Bishop Sweeten about it."

"I don't know. It's been a long time since I ..." His voice trailed off. "Stay here a minute."

He left the room and returned with a large painting of Sister Browning's parents.

"I painted it just like the photo she gave me," he said.

Sister Browning's parents looked angelic. I recognized the structure behind them in the background.

"What is that building?" Billy asked.

"It's the Salt Lake Temple," I said.

"Do you think she'll like the painting?" he asked us.

"Oh, yeah," I said. "That's really good."

That week Billy's dad took the painting to Primary to give to Sister Browning.

"I love it!" Sister Browning said. "Thank you so much. You did a great job. I knew you could do it. I'll write you a check."

Billy's dad shook his head. "You don't need to pay me for it. Take it as a gift. That's worth much more than money. I want to thank you for helping me realize that I could paint again."

Billy's dad started coming to church every week. Billy told me his dad met with the bishop weekly and began to make changes in his life. He stopped drinking. He even got a hair cut. Instead of his hair cascading down to his waist, it was clipped shoulder-length. While he kept his beard, he trimmed it, presumably with hedge clippers.

Eventually Billy's dad got a good job doing artwork for an advertising company in Los Angeles. That way, Billy's mom could quit her job and stay at home with Billy and be there when he got home from school.

Billy informed me that if his dad continued going to church and doing the things the bishop asked of him, he would be able to baptize him in December. Billy had waited that long, so what was a couple of more months? To me, Billy's dad being able to baptize him was a miracle that ranked right up there with Jesus walking on water.

CHAPTER 23

The Slumber Party

After spending countless hours reading together, Billy finished the Book of Mormon near the end of October—and I could verify that he read every word. I couldn't believe how his reading improved. Instead of stumbling over words all of the time, he got to where he could read quite smoothly. Phrases like "and it came to pass" and "for behold" just rolled off his tongue.

And, as promised, his mom paid him $50 for his efforts. She presented him with a card congratulating him on his feat and a $50 bill. To celebrate Billy's upcoming baptism, we thought it would be fun to have a slumber party. We had talked about it all summer, but it never happened. We knew it would take a lot of convincing on our part. It didn't seem possible that Danny's parents would let him, but we decided to give it a shot. We first needed to get the sleepover set up before we could invite him. I volunteered my house and I talked to my parents about it. I tried to help out around the house and got my homework done before dinner every night.

Finally, they said it would be okay.

When I told Billy, he asked his parents and they said he could come. My mom agreed to talk to Sister Rayford. She told my mom Danny had never slept over anywhere before without them and they were nervous about it. My mom promised that the boys would be safe and have a fun time together. When she got off the phone, my mom said Danny could come. I could hardly wait.

We decided to pitch a tent in our backyard and sleep out there. On the night of our party, we ate pizza and M&Ms and drank root beer. Then we went outside and played some games before retiring to our sleeping bags.

"Have fun out here," my mom said. "I'll leave the back door open in case you need to go to the bathroom."

We lay in our sleeping bags for a while, but we couldn't sleep. Using a flashlight, Billy told some ghost stories. I think Danny started getting scared because he had never spent a night away from home.

"Let's go visit Sister Browning," Billy said.

"Now?" I asked. "It's 10 o'clock."

Danny suggested we could give Sister Browning our extra pizza.

"Yeah, then we could toilet paper her yard," Billy said.

I had overheard Sister Browning tell my mom that she wanted to find a nice young man to date. I felt bad for Sister Browning. She was the best teacher we ever had. I thought it would be fun to surprise her and take her something to eat on a Friday night. We decided we could toilet paper her house, then clean it up in the morning.

It sounded like a good plan. I figured my parents were asleep, so I didn't bother waking them up and telling them what we were going to do. We quietly went through the back door and crept into the bathroom to grab a couple of rolls of toilet paper. Then I went into the kitchen and grabbed the box of cold pizza.

We wrote Sister Browning a note that said, "Thanks for being a great Primary teacher. From Billy, Danny and Kevin."

Tiptoeing through the entry, we put on our shoes, exited through the back door and left through the gate—dressed in pajamas. We walked down the street to her house.

A light was on inside, so we figured she was still awake. We placed the pizza and the note on the porch, then we started to toilet paper her yard. I kept telling Billy to be quiet because I thought he was making too much noise. Billy had Danny get on his shoulders and he lifted him up in the branch of a tree. While Danny was streaming the toilet paper, he leaned too far and fell about six feet onto the ground. He let out a loud yell and grabbed his ankle in pain. While we were trying to help him up, we heard police sirens blaring a few blocks away. The noise got closer and closer until, before we knew it, the police headlights were shining on us. Then I thought of my mom. I was more scared of my mom than of the police.

"What are you boys doing out here so late?" a police officer asked us.

"We're toilet papering our teacher's house," Billy said proudly.

"Your school teacher's?"

"No," I said, "our Primary teacher's."

Suddenly Sister Browning's front door flew open and she appeared on the porch, wearing a bathrobe and curlers in her hair.

"Oh my goodness," Sister Browning said as she inadvertently stepped on the pizza box. "I know these boys. They're in my class at church. I'm really sorry, officer."

Sister Browning had heard noises outside and she called the police, thinking we were burglars or something.

The police officer was not amused. "We're going to have to notify their parents of this," he said.

"It's okay, officer," Sister Browning said. "Let me call them."

While all this was going on, Brother Woodson's car pulled up to the house. He got out of the car, carrying a bouquet of flowers in his hand.

"What's going on?" he asked. "What are you boys doing here?"

"Brother Woodson, what are *you* doing here?" I asked.

"Sister Browning and I had a date scheduled for tonight, but she called and said she was sick. I thought I'd stop by. Isn't it past your bedtime? And what's with all the police cars?"

Billy couldn't resist making fun of Brother Woodson and Sister Browning. "Brother Woodson and Sister Browning, sitting in a tree, K-I-S-S-I-N . . ."

"Billy, you stop that," a red-faced Sister Browning said.

"They were toilet-papering this woman's house," the officer explained to Brother Woodson. "Do you know these boys, too?"

"Yeah," Brother Woodson said. "I'm sure they didn't mean any harm."

All of our parents came to Sister Browning's house. My mom was furious. She apologized to the police officer and to the other parents because we had left the house without her knowing.

Tension filled the night air. They saw the mess we had made all over Sister Browning's yard.

The Rayfords were very upset that their son, who they thought was safe and sound at my house, was actually out in the middle of the night. They became more angry when they found out Danny had injured his ankle.

"We finally let our son do something with friends and this is what happens," Sister Rayford said. She took her son by the arm and escorted him to her car. "I knew it would be a mistake. I've never seen such irresponsibility in all my life!"

My mom apologized profusely, but it didn't do much good.

For Billy's parents, this wasn't a big deal. They had been through plenty of incidents—much worse—with him before. His parents took him home, too.

Sister Browning tried to calm down all of the parents, but it was no use. I tried to explain that we were only trying to make Sister Browning happy.

"By scaring her half to death and messing up her yard?" Mom asked.

"We were planning to clean it all up in the morning," I said.

"You bet you are," my mom said. "And that's not all the work you'll be doing tomorrow."

That night I was on the receiving end of another lecture.

"Kevin, I don't understand why you like spending so much time with Billy."

"Mom, he's not as bad as you think," I said. "He's getting baptized, remember?"

"I remember," she said.

All in all, our slumber party was a disaster.

Kevin, I am so disappointed in you.

I couldn't erase the echo of those words from my ears. The last thing I wanted was to be a disappointment to my mom.

"If Billy Blankenship jumped off a cliff—which I could see him doing—would you do it, too?"

"No."

"Then why on earth do you do other things he tells you to do? He is a bad influence on you."

"Mom, it's not Billy's fault. It's mine. I'm the one that got the toilet paper."

I wanted to explain that, actually, I saw good in Billy, and tell her all the things he was doing, like reading scriptures and praying and writing in his journal, and remind her, again, how he was going to be baptized, but I knew that under the circumstances I should just keep my mouth shut.

"What kind of boy have I raised?" she asked. "I'm the Primary president and I've got the Rayfords mad at me. You used to be so obedient. You used to want to do what was right. What's gotten into you? I think Billy's gotten into you. And it's got to stop right now."

In the ten months since I started spending time with Billy, I had been in trouble more than the rest of my life combined. Ten months earlier, my parents were thrilled with me and Billy's parents were frustrated with him. Ten months later, Billy's parents thought they had the most wonderful son in the world while my parents acted like they wanted to turn me over to an orphanage.

During those ten months, I discovered that I actually liked Billy. I thought I should tell my parents about my assignment, but I just couldn't. Besides, it didn't seem like an assignment anymore.

As I sat in my bedroom, gazing up at the ceiling, I wondered why all of this was happening. All I was trying to do was help Billy come back to church and get baptized so he could receive the priesthood. We seemed to be making progress, but my parents were mad at me all of the time. I'd overhear my mom asking my dad, "Didn't we teach him to be stronger than that? Why can't he be more like his older brothers and sisters?"

"He needs to stay away from Billy," my dad would say. "Billy Blankenship's going to end up in jail one day."

My parents told me I was grounded "until further notice."

When Billy asked me over to his house, I told him I couldn't.

"I'm grounded," I said.

"Again?"

"Yeah."

"So you can't leave your house?"

"Yeah."

"Your parents are really mean. So can I come over to your house?"

I couldn't tell him that my parents banned me from playing with him ever again.

"I can't have any friends over, either," I said.

Spending a lot of time in my room alone gave me a lot of time to think—especially about turning 12 and receiving the priesthood. Given all of my run-ins with the law and the school principal that year, I was afraid that I would flunk my priesthood interview.

Every few nights, my dad would come into my room with his scriptures and begin a conversation about the priesthood. "Do you know what the oath and covenant of the priesthood is?" he asked me.

"No."

"When we get the priesthood, Kevin, that means we promise Heavenly Father that we will serve others and be obedient to the commandments. You understand that, don't you?"

"Yes, dad."

Then we read parts of D&C 20.

"Receiving the priesthood is a serious thing, Kevin," he said. "You're making a promise to Heavenly Father that you will obey your parents, do your best to help others and follow Jesus' example. Do you understand?"

"Yes, dad."

"Well, you had better think about this a little more before you turn 12. You've only got a few weeks to shape up."

"Okay, dad."

"Do you feel like you're ready to receive the priesthood?"

"I think I am," I said.

As of that moment, as I looked into my father's eyes, I remembered all the things that had happened: the water balloons at school, the window at the church shot out by a BB gun, and the toilet paper incident at Sister Browning's. I was certain they still thought I had stolen those football pencils, too.

Here my parents were, so worried about my willingness to keep the commandments. What they didn't know was, I *was* trying to keep the commandments and follow Jesus.

CHAPTER 24

490 Times

Skyler didn't share my excitement about Billy's impending baptism.

At church, Billy and I were talking to Sister Browning when Skyler asked her if Billy was really getting baptized.

"He is," Sister Browning said.

"And will he get the priesthood, too?"

"Yes, when he's ready."

"How can he? Do you remember what he did to my glasses? Do you remember all of the names he's called me?"

"Billy was interviewed by the bishop and found worthy to be baptized," said Sister Browning.

"That's not fair!" Skyler said, his face turning as red as a cherry tomato. "For years I've been doing everything right and he's done everything wrong. And he gets to be baptized, like me?"

Just then, Billy, who had overheard the exchange, walked toward us. "I'm sorry about your glasses, Skyler," Billy mumbled.

"See?" Sister Browning said. "Billy has shown that he wants to repent. That's one of the steps we must take before baptism."

"Yeah, but to repent, you have to make restitution. He hasn't done that," Skyler said.

"What's restitution?" Billy asked.

"It means you have to make up for the bad thing that you did. You broke my spectacles and they cost $79.95. If you don't repent, you can't get baptized, right, Sister Browning? Isn't that what Jesus taught?"

"Skyler," Sister Browning said, "Jesus taught that we should forgive others when they do things to us that make us mad. Jesus taught that we need to forgive '70 times seven times.'"

"Do you know how many times that is? That's 490 times!" Skyler said. "That's impossible. I'll bet I've forgiven him at least that many times already. I don't think he should be baptized. Or receive the priesthood. He's not worthy."

I noticed Billy turn and sullenly walk away.

"The bishop is the one who decides who is worthy," Sister Browning said. "What Billy just did took a lot of courage and faith. The Lord taught that we must forgive everyone, even when they don't apologize."

"I guess I can forgive Billy for breaking my spectacles," Skyler said, "but you don't know the rotten things he's done to me."

"Well, Skyler, that's the gospel," Sister Browning said. "We can repent and we can change. Billy has changed. He's not perfect. None of us are. But I've noticed great changes in him over the last several months."

"Billy can't change," Skyler said. "I bet after he gets baptized, he'll still do bad things."

"We all make mistakes, even after we get baptized," Sister Browning said. "But every time we do, if we have faith, repent and try to be more like Jesus, we will be forgiven."

I don't think that's what Skyler wanted to hear. He folded his arms and sulked.

"I've been doing all the right things my whole life. Billy has been doing all the wrong things his whole life. Now, all of the sudden, he gets to be baptized and get the priesthood? That's not fair. Letting him get baptized is a big mistake."

Later that day, Billy asked me to go with him to Skyler's palatial house.

"Billy, what are you going to do?" I asked. "Remember, you're getting baptized soon."

"I owe him," Billy said.

I tried to explain that revenge wasn't a good idea. Expecting a potentially ugly confrontation, I decided to go with him to act as an intermediary.

We walked up the long driveway, careful not to step on the Cherringtons' immaculately manicured lawn flanked by azaleas.

Billy rang the doorbell. It wasn't just a simple ringing sound. It played an elaborate classical music tune.

The imposing wooden door swung open. Sister Cherrington greeted us with a half-smile.

"Hello, boys. Is there something I can do for you?"

"Is Skyler here?" Billy asked.

Sister Cherrington paused for a moment. "May I ask what you need from him?"

"I have something for him."

A knuckle sandwich? I could practically read Sister Cherrington's mind. "Let me get him for you," she finally said.

Skyler lumbered to the entry, daring not to come within striking distance.

"What do you want?" he asked.

Billy stuffed his hand in his pocket and removed a $50 bill and handed it to Skyler.

"I'm sorry about your glasses. Here's some money. It's all I have. This is my restitution. I'll try not to do mean things to you anymore."

Skyler wore a look of shock on his corpulent face. "You probably stole this money," he said, examining the bill closely, holding it up to the light. "It's probably a counterfeit."

I knew where it came from, though. That was the money he had earned from reading the Book of Mormon. The gesture proved he actually learned something from what he had read.

"Is there something else you'd like to say to Billy, Skyler?" Sister Cherrington asked.

"Thanks," he said reluctantly.

I could tell Skyler was tortured inside. As much as Skyler complained about Billy, I think he liked having Billy around, just to have someone he could compare himself with and to make himself look better. It was as if Skyler enjoyed his role being the one who was picked on and teased by Billy. I think he realized those days were probably over.

That night the phone rang, and I was shocked to learn it was for me. I never got phone calls at 9 o'clock at night.

"Hello?" I said.

"Kevin? This is Billy. I wanted to call and tell you that the bishop said my dad is going to baptize me! Isn't that cool?"

I couldn't believe it. "Yeah," I said. "That is cool."

Yet another miracle.

CHAPTER 25

Billy's Baptism Day

After all these long months of moving out of my comfort zone, befriending Billy, praying for him dealing with his dad, making trips to the principal's office, getting in trouble with my parents, and getting grounded, the big day had finally arrived. All my hard work was paying off.

Billy was the only baptism scheduled in the stake that day. My family and I arrived at the church plenty early, as we were asked, and we sat quietly in the chapel. We listened to the organ play while we waited for the meeting to begin.

As I sat on the rock-hard pew, I flipped through the hymnbook.

"Israel, Israel, God is Calling *in the Bathroom*."

"I Saw A Mighty Angel Fly *in the Bathroom*."

"Let Zion in Her Beauty Rise *in the Bathroom*."

I thought of Billy and chuckled to myself.

Bishop Sweeten made his way from the back of the chapel to the pulpit. "Brothers and sisters, we have a situation to deal with," he said. "The Blankenships just called me and said that Eddie's boss told him that he was needed at work today. He told him about Billy's baptism, but his boss said he had to work to get a project done by this afternoon. It's pretty important. His boss told him to either show up at work or he'd be fired."

I knew that if Billy's dad got fired, Sister Blankenship would have to go back to work.

How much did one kid have to go through to get baptized? Billy had already waited this long. Now this.

The bishop said they made preliminary arrangements over the phone to wait until January for Billy to be baptized. I was bitterly disappointed. Everything was going so well, I should have known something else would go wrong.

Just before we stood up to leave, we saw Billy and his dad enter the chapel.

"It's not too late, is it?" Billy's dad asked.

"Of course not," the bishop said. "Did your boss change his mind?"

"No. After I got off the phone with you, I had a sick feeling. I knew I wasn't supposed to go to work. I called my boss back and asked him if I could come in later. He said no. I told him this day was too important to my son to miss. So I quit."

The bishop grabbed Brother Blankenship's hand. "You'll be blessed for putting the Lord first," he said.

I think Billy's dad earned everlasting respect from everyone in the ward for his decision. Billy and his dad excused themselves to change into their white baptismal clothing.

The bishop stepped to the pulpit again. "It seems we have another problem. There's some construction going on nearby and the water line has been cut. We have no water for the baptismal font. I'll try to contact some bishops in other wards in the area about holding the baptism in another building. It will delay us a while. I apologize for the inconvenience."

Of course. What else could go wrong?

The bishop got on the phone trying to find a solution.

While we waited, Sister Browning and Brother Woodson came up to my parents and me.

"Thank you for raising such a wonderful son," Sister Browning said to my mom and dad. "It's been a joy teaching him this year."

We looked at her left hand, where Sister Browning sported a brilliant diamond ring.

"Sister Browning," my mom said, "is there something you'd like to announce?"

She smiled and took Brother Woodson's hand. "Well," she said, "we got engaged last night."

My mom gasped, then gave Sister Browning a hug. "Congratulations! I'm so happy for you both! Kevin, isn't that exciting?"

"Yeah."

I still had a crush on Sister Browning. But I figured if I had to lose her to someone, it might as well be Brother Woodson, the man who was going to be my deacons quorum adviser.

"We'll be getting married in the Salt Lake Temple in the spring."

"Are you still going to be in our ward?" I asked.

"Of course," Brother Woodson said.

"Thank you for all you've done," my mom said. "You've worked miracles with these kids, especially Billy."

"Well, Kevin deserves the credit for that," Sister Browning said. Then she whispered, "If he hadn't taken on that special assignment I gave him, Billy wouldn't be here today."

"*Special assignment*?" Mom asked.

"Well, I guess it wasn't so much a special assignment as it was Kevin's willingness to do what the Lord would want him to do."

My mom looked puzzled.

"You mean Kevin never told you about that?" Sister Browning said.

"No, he didn't," my mom said, looking at me.

"Way back in January, I pulled Kevin aside after class and asked him to try to be a friend to Billy," she said. "He said he would so he could help Billy come back to church and get baptized."

"Well," my mom said, "that explains a lot."

Moments later, Sister Rayford and Danny approached me.

"Hi," I signed to Danny. He signed back with a smile.

"Thank you so much for being such a great friend to Danny," she said, becoming emotional. "You and Billy have been so kind to him. He loved playing baseball with you last summer. For the first time in his life he feels like he fits in."

Then she turned to my mom. "I'm sorry for the things I said at Sister Browning's house a while ago. I overreacted. We've talked a lot to Danny lately and we've realized we've been too controlling. We're going to let him do things that other kids his age do—except for toilet-papering houses at 11 o'clock at night. We're going to let him live life more. He can't spend his whole life locked in the house, reading books."

While Sister Rayford spoke, Billy and his dad returned to the chapel, dressed in white. It was quite a sight, one I wasn't sure I'd ever see.

By then, the bishop returned to the chapel with a discouraged look on his face. "We're still trying to find a church where we can do the baptisms," he said.

Billy raised his hand. "I know where we can do the baptisms," he said.

"Where?" the bishop asked.

"We've got a whole bunch of water just down the street."

"Yeah," Billy's dad said. "We've got the whole Pacific Ocean."

"The water may be a little cold, but that may be our best option," the bishop said. "Billy, are you okay with that?"

"Yeah!"

"Looks like you're getting your wish, being baptized in the ocean," I said to Billy.

It was a cool, overcast morning. Before going to the beach, we held the baptismal program in the chapel. It featured a talk by my mom on baptism and one by Billy's mom on the Holy Ghost.

Then Billy, Danny and I performed a musical number that we had rehearsed together. We sang, and signed, the words for, the Primary song, "Baptism."

Jesus came to John the Baptist
In Judea long ago,
And was baptized by immersion
In the river Jordan's flow.

We weren't very good singers, but we did our best. When I looked out into the congregation while we sang, a lot of people were wiping away tears.

We all left the church, loaded into our cars, and made a convoy to the beach—the same one where I had almost drowned months earlier.

We arrived and found the beach relatively deserted. Billy and his dad waded into the water until Billy was in chest-deep. Brother Woodson and the bishop served as the witnesses. Billy's dad lifted the stump of his right arm into the air and solemnly pronounced the words: "William Joseph Blankenship, having been commissioned of Jesus Christ, I baptize you in the name of the Father, and of the Son, and of the Holy Ghost. Amen."

Billy's dad plunged Billy into the water and lifted him out. Billy came up with a big smile on his face. Father and son embraced.

Afterward, the bishop gathered us all together again. "The scriptures say that after Jesus was baptized, 'the heavens were opened unto him, and he saw the Spirit of God descending like a dove, and lighting upon him.'"

I looked around. There were no doves on that day at the beach—but there was a flock of seagulls circling overhead.

"'And lo a voice from heaven, saying, This is my beloved Son, in whom I am well pleased,'" the bishop continued. "Well, I want you to know that I can imagine the voice of our Heavenly Father saying right now, 'This is Billy, in whom I am well pleased.'"

Before leaving, Billy, Danny and I posed for pictures on the beach. Danny and I were wearing white shirts and ties. Billy, soaking wet, was wearing his white baptismal clothes. We stood arm-in-arm together, grinning.

The following day during sacrament meeting, Brother Woodson confirmed Billy a member of the Church of Jesus Christ of Latter-day Saints.

Sister Browning deserved a lot of credit for Billy Blankenship's baptism. From the beginning she tried to have a good attitude about Billy. She must have decided that if she treated him like a good boy, then maybe he would act like one. After all, she was a woman of strong faith. She believed in miracles. And, sure enough, Billy Blankenship's baptism was a miracle. I had asked myself, "What in the world did she see in this kid?"

Well, it was certain that whatever she saw, it wasn't of this world. If it weren't for her, Billy Blankenship may have never been baptized.

CHAPTER 26

The Priesthood Interview

One night, I had a nightmare about my interview with the bishop. I walked into his office, which looked like a classroom at school, then I sat down at a desk. Bishop Sweeten dropped a thick test on the desk with all sorts of hard questions about the priesthood.

"You've got 10 minutes," the bishop said. "Begin."

I could feel my palms sweat as Bishop Sweeten paced around his office with a ruler. My mind went blank. Suddenly, he barked, "Time's up!" He picked up my half-finished test. He pulled out a red pen and marked it all up while shaking his head in disappointment.

"Kevin, you failed the priesthood test. You can try again next year. Your parents tell me you've been in detention and grounded for most of the school year . . ."

After I awoke, I studied feverishly for days to prepare for my priesthood interview, which was scheduled after church. All during sacrament meeting, I couldn't think of anything but that.

My parents and brothers and sisters waited outside for me as I walked into Bishop Sweeten's office.

"You've got a great missionary handshake," the bishop said.

"Thanks."

The bishop asked me to sit down in a hard, brown chair. Then he pulled his own chair, one with a soft cushion on the seat, over in front of me. He sat down, looked me in the eyes and smiled.

"Kevin, how have you been?"

"Fine."

"Do you know why you're meeting with me today?"

"Yes."

"Would you like to tell me?"

"Well, I'm here because I want to get the priesthood."

"Why do you want to get the priesthood?"

It was the same question Billy Blankenship had asked me a few months earlier.

"I want to receive the priesthood because I want to follow Jesus and serve others," I said.

The bishop's eyes twinkled. "That's the best answer I've ever heard to that question," he said. "Are you ready to receive the priesthood?"

I started to say yes, then I stopped. "Well, I don't know."

Then I told him everything that had happened over the course of the past year.

"But," I added, "I am trying to be like Jesus."

Bishop Sweeten nodded. "Yes," he said. "I know you are."

"How do you know that?" I asked.

"Because I'm the bishop. I know things like that. More importantly, Heavenly Father knows, too."

Suddenly, I felt this warm, peaceful feeling envelop me. Right then, something told me that everything I had learned at church was true. More than ever, I knew that I needed the priesthood. I couldn't wait.

A couple of weeks after Billy's baptism, Billy, Danny and I received the priesthood—on the same December day. I was ordained a deacon by my dad and Danny was ordained by his dad. Brother Woodson ordained Billy.

On the first Sunday after we received the priesthood, the three of us passed the sacrament for the first time. Billy was nervous and I couldn't blame him. Everyone watched every move he made. They were shocked to see him acting in that capacity and they didn't know what he'd do next. To everybody's surprise, Billy carried out his duty with dignity.

Around the following Easter, Brother Blankenship and Billy showed up at our house. Brother Blankenship stood on the porch holding a large, rectangular-shaped package, wrapped in brown paper and a ribbon. I invited Billy and his dad inside.

"This is for you, Kevin," Brother Blankenship said. "This is my way of saying thank you for all you've done for me and Billy and our family."

I tore off the wrapping. Underneath was a beautiful painting of Billy, Danny and me, standing on the beach on Billy's baptismal day.

"I painted one for Billy and one for Danny just like it," Brother Blankenship said. "I hope it will help each of you remember that special day."

"Are you sure we can't pay you anything for this?" Dad asked. "For your time? For the frame? We really owe you."

Brother Blankenship smiled and shook his head. "Absolutely not. I owe you."

By this time my mom walked into the room.

"This gift is out of gratitude for what Kevin has done for us," Brother Blankenship continued. "Billy and Kevin don't know this, but last summer I would be at home, feeling sorry for myself, and I'd hear Billy and Kevin in Billy's room, reading from the Book of Mormon and saying their prayers and talking about baptism. I hadn't been to church in years. But to hear them talk, it did something to my heart."

My mom and dad were confused.

"They read scriptures at your house?" Mom asked.

"Yeah, almost every day. Didn't you know that?"

My mom looked at me again. "No," she said, gently placing

her hands on my shoulders. Her eyes moistened.

"They had this little deal. Kevin taught Billy to read and Billy taught Kevin to swim. They spent most of the summer helping each other. Then I'd see how Kevin treated Billy. He was a real friend to my son. You know how it says in the scriptures that 'A little child shall lead them?' Well, that's what happened. I owe everything to these boys. They motivated me to return to the Church and to become worthy to baptize my son."

As I watched Billy and his dad leave our house that night and disappear down the street, I realized it was worth all that I had gone through trying to be one of the Lord's shepherds. What had started as a "special assignment" from Sister Browning had resulted in a miraculous change in the lives of a boy and his father.

Dad helped me hang the painting up in my bedroom, and my parents told me how proud they were of me for helping Billy.

"Thanks," Mom said, hugging me tightly, "for being a great example of what it means to follow the Savior."

CHAPTER 27

"Demon Deacon"

The only bad thing I could think of about becoming a deacon was that Sister Browning wouldn't be my teacher anymore.

She and Brother Woodson were married in the Salt Lake Temple that spring, as planned. After their honeymoon to Hawaii, they returned home and held a reception at the church. Brother and Sister Woodson asked all of us in the deacons quorum to help out at the reception for those in our ward.

We set up chairs, served refreshments and emptied the garbage.

True, Billy had been recently baptized, had recently received the Aaronic priesthood, and had matured in amazing ways in the previous years. Still, people wondered how long it would last. I overheard one adult say that Billy would be the ward's "Demon Deacon."

True to form, Billy couldn't resist instigating a little trouble. He removed the whipped cream off the pies being served and replaced them with shaving cream that he brought with him from home. Sister Wilkins just about threw up when she took a bite.

Somehow Billy wound up with Sister Woodson's garter. He used it as a slingshot, flinging eclairs at unsuspecting reception guests.

"Billy," Brother Woodson smiled, looking uncomfortable in his black tuxedo, "I don't know whether to slug you or hug you."

Despite Billy's best attempt at ruining the reception, Brother and Sister Woodson looked really happy. They seemed to belong together.

Several months after I received the priesthood, I was sustained and set apart as the deacons quorum president.

"Billy, you're a great example in our quorum," Brother Woodson told me. "You'll be a great president."

I hoped I would be. I called Billy to serve as quorum secretary. While he performed his duties well, he always stirred up trouble.

During one Scout meeting, Billy showed me the contents of his coat pockets. He had about a dozen eggs in there.

"What are those for?" I asked.

"Shhhhhh!" Billy said. "We're going to have some fun when this is over."

While we walked home from the church that night, he stopped at the Jones' house and climbed up a tall tree.

"C'mon up!" he said.

"Why? What are you doing?"

"We're egg-bombing cars!"

"Bad idea," I told him.

"It's fun."

"Billy, we're Boy Scouts and deacons. I don't feel good about it . . ."

"Why? Just because you're the president? C'mon, Prez!"

I hated it when he called me that. "We're going to get in trouble," I said.

"Hey, how do you like your eggs?"

"Scrambled," I said.

"Scrambled? Okay, watch!"

A car passed by and suddenly I heard a thud. An egg smashed into the drivers' side door. The car screeched to a halt. Guilty by association, I ran and hid in the nearby bushes.

The driver of the car searched for a good 10 minutes for the perpetrators before leaving in disgust. I just sat in the bushes, shivering in the cold, wishing I was home.

By the time Billy ran out of eggs, I didn't want to go home. I knew my mom and dad would be waiting up for me, wondering where I was. I had promised them I'd be home right after scouts. I was already 45 minutes late.

Not only was I grounded for a week, but I also was on the receiving end of a harrowing harangue from my dad. He sternly lectured me about the priesthood.

"You're supposed to be an example to the rest of the deacons," he said.

"I'm sorry, dad," I said.

I did my best to channel Billy's boundless energy for good. And sometimes I succeeded.

Bishop Sweeten called Billy's dad to serve an assistant Scoutmaster. He went with us on campouts and worked with us on merit badges.

A couple of months before Christmas, our Boy Scout troop organized a fund raiser to earn money for summer camp. We received a shipment of hundreds of first aid kits that we planned to sell door-to-door throughout the neighborhood. A contest was organized, where we were paired off and the duo that sold the most first aid kits could pick whatever they wanted out of the Scouting catalog. I had my eye on a new, goose-feathered sleeping bag; Billy wanted a Swiss Army knife.

Naturally, Skyler's dad bought a whole box of first aid kits himself. Right off the bat, we were all way behind him. But we were determined to win the contest.

We asked Billy's dad to take us to a rich neighborhood, near the Cherringtons' house, and drop us off for an afternoon. These people had money and we wanted to squeeze a little bit out of them. Dressed in our full Scout uniforms, we decided to take turns selling. I was first. We walked up the stairs and I nervously knocked on the front door. An elderly woman opened it.

"Excuse me, ma'am, my name is Kevin and this is Billy," I began. "We are Boy Scouts trying to earn money for summer camp. Would you like to buy a first-aid kit?"

"Can't you read?" the woman asked us, pointing at a metal sign attached to the door.

"Yes," I said.

"Then what does this say?"

"No Soliciting."

"What does that mean?" Billy asked.

"It means go away." With that, she slammed the door.

I felt like crying. I wanted to go home.

"Your approach is wrong," Billy said. "Watch me."

At the next house, Billy laid down on the lawn.

"What are you doing?" I asked. "This is no time to rest. We've got a whole box of first-aid kits to sell."

"Just stand there and look worried," he said. I had no idea what Billy was doing.

Reaching into his pocket, he pulled out a packet of ketchup, one of those you get at a fast food restaurant, opened it and spread the red condiment all over his forehead.

Before I could ask him again what he was doing, he began screaming hysterically and convulsing.

Within minutes, a crowd of people rushed toward us. A man bent down, lifting Billy's head slightly. "Somebody call 9-1-1!" he yelled.

"Wait!" Billy exclaimed, rising to his feet. People gasped. I think one woman fainted.

"Son, lay down. You're bleeding badly," the man said.

"It's okay," Billy assured him. Then he took his finger and removed the red liquid and stuck it in his mouth.

"It's only ketchup," he said.

I was certain the people would injure him for real at that point. But Billy wasn't done yet.

"I'm sorry to scare you," he said. "But this was just an example of what could happen if you're not prepared. Something like this could happen to you or someone in your family. The Scout motto is 'Be Prepared.' That's why we're here today, to help you be prepared."

I looked around and he had a captive audience, listening to every word. Billy removed a first-aid kit from the box and lifted it in the air for all to see.

"For just $7, you can have your own first-aid kit. We're helping people to be prepared. Plus, you'll be helping us go to summer camp."

"It's a great tax write-off," I added.

Before we knew it, most of those people returned to their homes and brought back cash and their check books. In a matter of minutes, we sold all of our first-aid kits.

Now, up until that moment, I never thought I would say "Billy Blankenship" and "genius" in the same paragraph, let alone the same sentence. But it was pure genius. He was a natural-born salesman. For the first time, I remember thinking that he might make a good missionary.

Since I was more responsible than Billy, I assigned myself the task of carrying the money. I relished being the caretaker of large sums of cash, even if it didn't belong to me.

By the end of the month, Billy and I sold 11 boxes of first-aid kits, using various selling tactics. We outsold Skyler and his companion, who sold only six. I got my sleeping bag and Billy got his Swiss Army knife.

Though I was proud of the accomplishment, I realized I was simply riding Billy's coattails. He had sold so many first-aid kits, the Red Cross would have been proud. If he were a girl, he would have set a world record for selling Girl Scout cookies.

Billy also came in handy when we played in the annual stake basketball tournament. He nearly single-handedly took us to the championship game. Our biggest problem was making sure he didn't foul out.

Billy also was eager to do service projects, even ones that weren't required for the Eagle Scout Award. In our ward lived a widow named Sister Tewksbury. She was a shut-in, unable to attend church or go anywhere else. We'd go to her house on Sundays with a member of the bishopric to administer the sacrament to her, then we'd visit with her for 20 minutes. Invariably she'd tell us how she wished she was healthy enough to go outside and pull the weeds in her yard.

One day after school I asked Billy if he wanted to go swimming but he said he was going to be busy. He told me he was going to Sister Tewksbury's house and pull her weeds.

As the deacons quorum president, I felt badly that I hadn't thought of that first. So we spent two or three hours on our knees in the dirt beautifying Sister Tewksbury's yard. At one point, we saw her looking out the window, smiling and waving. I noticed tears flowing down her face.

Billy smiled and waved back.

Not bad for a demon deacon, huh?

CHAPTER 28

Life Goes On

It's hard to believe that all happened some 30 years ago. So much has transpired since then.

Looking back, I see that my prayers asking Heavenly Father to send an angel to change Billy were answered. I believe Danny Rayford was sent to our Primary class to help Billy get baptized. No one else in the world could have softened Billy's heart like he did.

Danny's time in our ward helped him, too, I think.

A few weeks after Billy's baptism, his parents removed him from private school and enrolled him in our public school. He was put in Mrs. Perkins' class with Billy and me. Billy acted like his older brother, but Danny learned how to fend for himself. Danny's parents started allowing him to come to our houses and they became less overprotective of him. They let him ride bikes around the neighborhood with us. By late summer, though, the military transferred Danny's dad to Maryland and the Rayfords moved away. We wrote letters to him for a few months, then we lost track of him.

Many years later, my parents were called to serve a mission in Chicago. That's where they saw Danny Rayford, grown up with a wife and five children. He was Dr. Daniel Rayford, an orthopedic surgeon and a member of a deaf branch presidency.

Skyler Cherrington went on to be the valedictorian of our high school. The summer before his sophomore year, he traded in his "spectacles" for contacts and, as time went on, he became a little more humble. Skyler turned out to be a good guy. Billy and I actually became friends with him and we all attended seminary together. He later graduated from Harvard. Today he's an optometrist living in San Diego.

After he got fired from his graphic design job, Billy's dad wasn't unemployed for long. Someone in our ward hired him as an artist, creating billboards. What he enjoyed doing most was religious paintings. He sold many of them and ended up donating a bunch of portraits of Christ to our ward, and to this day they are hanging on the walls of the church that I attended as a kid. Today, a couple of his artistic renderings adorn the walls of the Church's Conference Center in Salt Lake City.

About the time I advanced to the teachers quorum, Brother and Sister Woodson moved away. Billy and I were saddened to see them leave, but Brother Woodson got a new job as a CEO of a company in northern California. The Woodsons sent us a photo of their first child. It was a boy. Maybe it was coincidence, but they named him Kevin.

As we got older, Billy and I became even closer friends. We started swimming together down at the local rec center, in an Olympic-sized pool, on a regular basis. My parents thought it would be good for me to ensure that I would never again be afraid of the water. Billy's parents wanted him to do it as an outlet to release all of his nervous energy. While I did it for fun, Billy aspired to be an Olympic swimmer. He wanted to be standing on a podium someday with the national anthem playing in the background and a gold medal dangling from his neck.

"I want to be on a box of Wheaties, like Mark Spitz," Billy told me. "*Wheaties: The Breakfast of Champions!*"

Billy made the swim team as a sophomore. He was considered "a jock," but he wasn't really one of them because didn't act like a jerk or drink alcohol like many of them did. Billy would simply tell people he was a Mormon and that he didn't drink. So instead of attending their wild parties on the weekends, he and I would usually hang out at the church and play basketball. When he went to events where alcohol was served, he stood up for his beliefs by drinking a large glass of milk.

By our senior year, Billy became the star of the swim team and he won the state championship in the 100-meter breaststroke and 100-meter fly. When reporters or teammates would ask him the secret to his success, he'd say, "Practicing a lot and drinking a lot of milk."

In high school, we both worked hard in the classroom. In fact, we often did homework together. I wasn't the best student, but I realized if I were to possess the finer things in life, I needed to do well in school. My goal was to make my first million dollars by the time I was 30.

Billy and I attended Seminary together, and, as a senior, I was called to be the seminary president. We woke up at 5 a.m. every morning to go to class, then Billy rushed off to swim practice.

In school, Billy made the honor roll—amazing for a kid who learned in high school that he had been battling dyslexia since elementary school. It was too bad that Billy's dad wasn't alive to see him accomplish all of that. He died of heart failure when Billy and I were in the ninth grade. Before his death, he was serving in the Sunday School presidency in our ward and working once a week at the Los Angeles Temple.

When the 1984 Summer Olympics came to Los Angeles, just after our sophomore year of high school, we watched as much as we could. Somehow we were able to get tickets to some of the swimming events, which was a highlight for Billy. He had it all figured out—he would train hard to prepare for the 1988 Olympics in Seoul, South Korea.

I knew that by 1988 I would be serving a mission somewhere. Billy didn't really talk about serving a mission. He continued training hard and he attracted the attention of plenty of college recruiters. He wanted to stay close to home to be near his mom, but she told him he had to do what was best for him. Eventually, he accepted a swimming scholarship to the University of Michigan.

After graduation we went our separate ways. I enrolled at a local community college and started taking classes and he enrolled at Michigan. When he came home during Christmas break his freshman year, he told me that he had decided to serve a mission. Billy said when he told the coaches, they were very upset. Billy apologized, but said he felt a mission was something he needed to do. They said if he left, they would revoke his scholarship.

Billy was not only giving up on his scholarship, he was also giving up his Olympic dream.

He went to Bolivia on his mission. I was called to Florida. We wrote each other almost weekly during those two years and when we returned from our missions, it was like being in high school again. We both enrolled at Cal-State Northridge and were roommates for two years, until we each met wonderful girls and got married in the Los Angeles Temple within a month of each other.

Those college years were tough—scrimping, saving and eking out a meager existence. My wife and I lived in an austere apartment near campus with leaky faucets and a bevy of rodents. She worked long hours as a bank teller, and I vowed that one day our sacrifices would pay off. I promised her that we'd live in a comfortable house and that money would be the least of our troubles.

Billy and I even graduated together. He got a degree in advertising; I earned one in accounting. Our wives had babies within two weeks of each other. When I stood in the circle while he blessed his baby girl, I was proud.

After graduation, Billy landed a job at a big advertising agency in Los Angeles and I pursued a master's degree in accounting. I went on to get my master's degree and I became a CPA. I received a job offer from a big firm on the East Coast. Not to brag, but I was told I was hired over some Ivy League graduates. I felt so blessed. My little family left southern California and settled in Boston.

Billy and I both got busy with our jobs and our growing families, but we'd talk occasionally on the phone. He told me that his company turned over an account for a major beer company to him, but he declined, explaining that he was a Mormon and did not drink alcohol and that he didn't want to be involved in selling something he didn't believe in. The executives nearly fired him for that, but, in the end, they respected his wishes.

Billy, who grew up as a television addict, was a natural in advertising. When we used to watch TV together in high school, he'd analyze ads and tell me stuff I had never thought of. After our missions, he said President Spencer W. Kimball deserved the credit for the hugely popular "Just do it" ad campaign launched by Nike, the giant shoe manufacturer.

"They stole that line from President Kimball!" he told me. "That was his motto: 'Do It!'"

Soon Billy became a wealthy and successful corporate executive. Living on opposite coasts in high-pressure jobs, he and I both worked long hours. We stopped talking on the phone. After a while, the only communication was limited to the yearly exchange of Christmas cards.

CHAPTER 29

Fall In New England

I liked my job, but it required that I work brutal hours. I'd get to work at 5 o'clock in the morning and I didn't get home until 10 o'clock most nights. It seemed like I'd go for weeks without seeing my family, especially during tax season.

Occasionally I'd be asked to take trips overseas to Europe and Asia, helping to shore up foreign subsidiaries. I missed my daughter's first steps and my son's second birthday, among other things.

We lived in a cramped apartment in Boston and we tried to save money so we could move to the suburbs, into a nice house for our growing family, which included three young children. Everything in the Boston area was expensive, so I knew it would take a while.

Frustration mounted. After nine years of trying to save money for a nice house—I wanted to hold out for one with a swimming pool—we had little to show for our sacrifices. Plus, I was gone so much, even on Sundays, that I stopped going to church. At first I justified it, figuring Heavenly Father would understand, because I was working so hard the rest of the week trying to provide for my family. But I stopped doing other things I knew I was supposed to be doing, like reading the scriptures, saying my prayers, paying my tithing. My job crowded out all the things that had once been so important in my life.

My co-workers, many of whom did not have children, were

constantly talking about taking exotic vacations with their wives and putting a swimming pool in the backyard. Me? I felt like I was treading water financially, and gradually sinking.

Feeling guilty about being away from my wife and children so much, I started charging things to my credit card. Flowers for my wife, toys for the children. I wanted them to be happy and I thought that would make up for the void of me not being at home much. My wife would question me about my purchases, but I told her spending a little here and there wouldn't hurt. Credit card companies were handing cards out like candy, so it wasn't hard. I maxed out all of the cards I could get my hands on. Being an accountant, I knew better than to get into massive debt, but I figured I had no other choice. The credit card bills were sent to my work address so that my wife wouldn't worry about it. She had enough to deal with raising our children.

Someone at work told me about a parcel of land in the Boston suburbs for sale. It was the perfect spot for my wife and I to build our dream house. I didn't want to tell her about it, though, because I didn't want to get her hopes up. I wanted to pay it off, then surprise her and let her be in charge of the plans for the house. So I decided to purchase the lot. It wasn't cheap.

Trouble was, I didn't have the money to pay for the property.

At work I frequently handled large accounts, and it occurred to me that I could take a relatively small amount of money—small enough that it wouldn't be noticed—and pay off my credit cards before anyone knew the money was gone. I allowed the idea to play in my mind for several weeks. At first, I dismissed it completely. Soon, as I kept entertaining that thought, it sounded like the right solution to my financial woes.

This is what I did: I fraudulently billed my company for services rendered, then wrote a check to a fake business that I invented. I had found a weakness in the system and I exploited it.

I rationalized to myself that I was just borrowing the money.

With that secret account, I funneled money into it for my own purposes. After a while, I had diverted $120,000 into my phony business. Once I caught up on my debts, I decided to continue doing it so I could buy that piece of land. Over a matter of a few months, I had enough built up that I was able to do it.

In time, I thought, I would pay it all back without anybody noticing.

Of course, such actions went against everything I had been taught. But this was a $650 million company. They wouldn't miss a little bit of that money, right? It wasn't really stealing, I told myself, because I would pay it back in full before anyone knew the money was missing. This money, I thought, would remove so much stress from my life.

However, I realized that quite the opposite occurred. My actions only increased the stress in my life. My account had been filled, but my soul felt empty. I continued to justify my behavior, telling myself I was merely borrowing the money for a short time. Still, I couldn't bring myself to tell my wife about the purchase until I paid it all off. But paying it off seemed increasingly more difficult. It would take years.

I started living my life looking over my shoulder, scared to death that someone might find out about my duplicitous actions. I had trouble sleeping at night. My wife would ask me what was wrong and I blamed it on insomnia.

During this period I felt like I was shrouded in darkness. I found no joy in anything. I blamed it on a mid-life crisis.

In truth, I was abusing my position of trust within the company. I knew it had to stop. When I decided to come forward, I felt an initial sense of peace, even though I knew that I would have to pay for what I had done.

Sweat covered my body. I felt like throwing up. My heart pounded. I went into a bathroom stall at work and I quietly cried.

What had I done? I knew what I had done was wrong and I saw what it had done to me.

That night, I was trembling as I drove home. I had let down my company, my wife, my family, the Church, the Lord. I felt like a complete failure. I kept asking myself how I could have sunk to such a low point.

After the kids went to sleep, I told my wife what I had done. I think she went through the denial and anger stages all in one night. At first, she was shocked that I would do such a thing. Then she got mad. She wept uncontrollably. I wasn't sure if she'd ever want to see me again. I apologized, but the words rung hollow. I had jeopardized everything that was important to me. I had betrayed the ones that I loved. My life had unraveled.

I called the bishop of the ward and he agreed to see me. He was a kind man, but he felt like stranger to me because it had been so long since I had gone to church. I confessed to him what I had done and he cried with me, too. I knew what I needed to do. I didn't sleep at all that night.

Early the next morning, I arrived at work and knocked on my boss's door. Although I had already told my wife and my bishop, telling my boss what I had done was no easier. I apologized and told him, more than anything, I wanted I could go back in time and undo what I had done. He also expressed shock and disappointment.

But what really stung was when he said, "Kevin, the reason why we hired you over those other applicants years ago was because you were a Mormon. I thought you Mormons were trustworthy and honest."

Those words pierced my heart.

"We are," I said. "I was not practicing what I believe."

"If you needed money, why didn't you ask for a raise?" he asked, taking a sip of coffee.

"I guess I should have."

"You know what this means."

I nodded.

"As much as I like you, Kevin, I'm going to have to terminate you immediately and get the police involved. We've had some problems before with this in our company. I am disappointed. You were one of the hardest working, most dedicated employees I've ever had. But I have no other choice than to press charges. That's the company policy in cases such as this."

"Sir, I understand," I said, "I'll turn myself in. And I will pay back all the money I took, with interest. I promise."

My boss called security and I was escorted outside. Within a few minutes, a few boxes of my office possessions were loaded into my car. It was difficult explaining to my children that I had made a mistake and that I would be going away for a while. I had promised my parents as a kid that I'd always tell them what was going on in my life, and I told them about my mistake. They were distraught, too.

The company had taken out a crime insurance policy years earlier. Ironically, I had helped set up that policy. The insurance covered the theft, but that didn't make me feel any better.

I contacted a lawyer friend of mine. A week later I attended a hearing and pled guilty to embezzlement. The judge sentenced me to two months at the county jail, a place where a lot of white-collar criminals, like me, were serving time. He ordered me to pay back the money, which I had already planned to do.

Going to jail, I had to tell my children, was the consequence of poor choices I had made. I expressed my love for them and begged for their forgiveness. The look of disappointment on my kids' faces, knowing how I had been a bad example, almost destroyed me.

My son, McKay, was almost seven years old and a year away from his baptism. More than anything, I wanted to be worthy to be able to baptize him, just as my dad had baptized me. I feared

I wouldn't be able to do that. I feared I would lose my family forever. I had thrown everything that I held dear away. And for what? Money? Suddenly, money seemed totally unimportant. I learned what was meant by Godly sorrow.

After all the Lord had given me, I had let Him down. I had let everyone in my life down—my parents, my wife, my children. Telling my mom what had happened was grueling, much more than telling her about water balloons thrown from the roof of the school or shooting out a window at the church.

Kevin, I am so disappointed in you.

My mom didn't say those words when I told her about my crime, but I knew that's what she was thinking.

CHAPTER 30

Going Home

That first night in my jail cell, dressed in an ugly, loose-fitting orange jumpsuit, I opened one of the few possessions I was allowed to bring with me: the Book of Mormon. I had gone months and months without reading it. Sadly, I couldn't even remember the last time I had opened the book. As I read the familiar words, they comforted me like an old friend. At the same time, those words seared my conscience. Why didn't I just keep the commandments, like I had been taught?

It wasn't until I was no longer worthy, through my actions, to be a priesthood holder that I felt the loss of that priesthood power. What I wouldn't have given to simply be a deacon again.

I could relate to Alma the Younger in the Book of Mormon, who was racked with eternal torment for the sins he had committed. But while in this condition, Alma said, *"I remembered also to have heard my father prophesy unto the people concerning the coming of one Jesus Christ, a Son of God, to atone for the sins of the world."*

"Now, as my mind caught hold upon this thought, I cried within my heart: O Jesus, thou son of God, have mercy on me, who am in the gall of bitterness, and am encircled about by the everlasting chains of death.

"And now, behold, when I thought this, I could remember my pains no more; yea, I was harrowed up by the memory of my sins no more.

"And oh, what joy, and what marvelous light I did behold, yea, my soul was filled with joy as exceeding as was my pain!"

As I read those words over and over, I began to regain hope that I could someday work my way back to where I had once been.

My parents wanted to come visit me and my family, but mom suffered from a severe case of arthritis and couldn't travel. My wife didn't even visit me; it was too upsetting for her. I talked to her and the children on the phone once a week. I didn't want the kids to visit me because I didn't want them to see me that way.

One Sunday afternoon, when the warden came and said I had some visitors, I was surprised and curious. I certainly wasn't expecting anyone. I figured maybe it was my bishop, or my home teachers, who continued to visit me every week. I was ushered into the visiting room.

Sitting there were two familiar faces from my past: an older couple dressed in their Sunday best. I was shocked to see them and ashamed that they had to see me like this.

"Kevin," they chorused, "it's so good to see you."

As I got closer to them, I saw they were wearing nametags.

His nametag read, "President Woodson, The Church of Jesus Christ of Latter-day Saints."

"Are you missionaries?" I asked.

"Yes. I'm the new president of the Boston Massachusetts Mission. But I'm not here in that capacity," Brother Woodson said. "I'm here as your deacons quorum advisor. I'll always be your deacons quorum advisor."

"And I will always be your Primary teacher," Sister Woodson said.

Decades had passed since I had last seen the Woodsons. I noticed the gray in their hair, the wrinkles around their eyes. But that same, familiar light I remembered them having years earlier still shown from their countenances. They asked about my family and told me they had six children and 11 grandchildren.

Feeling uncomfortable, I finally blurted it out. "I'm so sorry to disappoint you." I felt like I was 11 years old all over again.

"Kevin, you are a child of God," Sister Woodson said. "He loves you. No matter what you do, He will always love you. We love you, too."

There were no lectures, no preaching. As always, Sister Woodson knew exactly what to say. Brother Woodson's baseball analogy of returning home flashed in my mind and I knew at that point in my life, I was way out in left field, and I longed to return home, literally and figuratively.

"And there's someone else we brought with us today," Sister Woodson said.

On cue, entering the room sporting meticulously trimmed hair and dressed in a navy blue suit, was Billy Blankenship. He had come all the way from California to visit me. We embraced.

"Thank you for coming," I said, shedding tears on Billy's lapels. "It's great to see you again."

"It's been a long time."

"Too long. I'm just sorry it has to be like this."

"Billy has recently been called to serve as a bishop," Sister Woodson informed me. Billy Blankenship was now Bishop William J. Blankenship.

"Can you believe that?" Billy said.

"Bishop, huh?" I said. "I can't wait to get out of here, just to watch you conduct a sacrament meeting."

Billy smiled and said, "Our opening hymn will be 'How Firm A Foundation *in the Bathroom*.'"

With tears still in our eyes, we laughed.

"I can't believe you came all of this way," I said.

"That's what friends do."

"I'm so embarrassed. I don't know what to say."

"You don't need to explain anything. I came out here to thank you."

"Thank me?"

"You know, when your parents tracked me down and told me what had happened, I started thinking about our friendship over the years. I realized that I had never thanked you."

"For what?"

"For being an example to me."

"Some example," I said, tugging on my orange jumpsuit.

Then it all came rushing back to my mind—that day some 30 years earlier when we stood at the beach, posing in a photo, with Danny and I wearing white shirts and ties, and Billy dressed in white baptismal clothing. Orange was a long way from white on the eternal color wheel.

"Kevin, if it weren't for you, I don't know where I'd be today. You were my first real friend. You encouraged me to go to church. You took the blame for me when I did things that were wrong. To this day, you stand as the best example of the Lord I have ever seen. Nobody had ever done anything like that for me. You helped me overcome a lot that summer before I was baptized by being patient with me, by reading the Book of Mormon with me. You helped me learn that I could read, that I could be successful in school.

"It was because of you, because of your example that I decided to get baptized and get the priesthood. It's because of you that I have such a strong testimony of the Lord. You gave me the courage to ask my dad to baptize me and he was able to return to the Church and receive all the blessings of the gospel. Now we'll be an eternal family, because of you.

"In high school you gave me the courage to go to seminary and tell people I was Mormon. I never told you this, but it was because of you I decided to go on a mission. I wanted so bad to be in the Olympics, but when I went to Michigan, I realized I didn't want to be like any of my Olympic heroes anymore. Growing up, you were a billboard for the kind of person I wanted to be. I wanted to be like you."

Chills covered my body. I couldn't see Billy through my tears.

"When we were young kids, you helped me. Now allow me to return the favor. A long time ago, we learned from Sister Browning, um, Woodson, to be willing to bear one another's burdens and to mourn with those who mourn and comfort those that stand in need of comfort. You made a mistake. You stuck with me when I made mistakes. I don't feel any differently about you now then I did before. I know the kind of person you are. You taught me about faith, repentance, baptism. You also taught me that the Lord will forgive us when we make mistakes. Growing up, you were the strong one. Now let me be strong for you."

Billy put his arm around me.

"I've got something to tell you, too," I said, glancing at Sister Woodson.

"What?"

"You should probably know that Sister Browning, um, Sister Woodson, was the one who asked me to befriend you and help you return to Church."

Billy smiled. "I know all about being a 'project.' I'd say nobody in the history of the Church has fulfilled an assignment better. Only a kid that had been put up to it—or had a death wish—would have tried to be my friend back then."

"How did you know about the assignment? Who told you?"

"Nobody. Nobody had to. Even back then, I knew there weren't any kids who would have wanted to be my friend on their own. It took me a while to believe that you were sincere about being my friend. You cared about me at a time when few people did. That's all that I wanted—acceptance and love, no matter what I did."

"Kind of like what I need now," I said.

Listening to Billy talk, it hit me that the kid that everybody in our ward used to think was destined for jail someday was just visiting. I was the one in jail. Who would have guessed it?

"I love you like a brother," Billy said. "I want you to know that I'm fasting and praying for you."

When visitors' hours were up, the three of them left. I felt as though I had been personally visited by the Three Nephites. I was even more resolved to change my life.

After all those years of going to Primary, attending seminary and serving a mission, I knew that Jesus Christ was my savior. I had testified that I believed it many times. I had heard, and had taught, many parables about the Atonement. But inside that lonely, bleak jail cell, the Savior and His Atonement became a reality to me. I understood why living the gospel is the only way to true peace and happiness in this life.

CHAPTER 31

A Changed Man

When my two-month sentence was over, I was released from jail and I can say I was a changed man. My love for the Savior, and for my family, increased profoundly. My wife forgave me for the pain I had caused her and the children. I had paid my debt to society, but I knew that I would always be indebted to the Savior.

President and Sister Woodson wanted to meet my family, so they invited us to go to a Red Sox game at Fenway Park on a Monday night for Family Home Evening. He taught my kids the baseball analogy he had taught me years earlier.

"Baseball is a microcosm of life. In baseball, the goal is to score runs, to get back to where we started from—home plate. But there are obstacles in our way—the pitcher and the fielders. We have to use everything we have, our eyes, our feet, our arms, our legs, and our heads to make our way around the bases. Luckily, we have those bases to keep us safe. We have coaches at first and third bases, guiding us.

"In life, it's the same thing. We're trying to return home—a heavenly home. To get there, we have a lot of things to overcome. We need to try our best and use the 'bases' the Lord has given us, like scriptures, the priesthood, and the commandments so we can be safe. We need to listen to our leaders who guide us. If we do, we can make it back to our heavenly home."

The land I had purchased with my company's money I sold at

a marginal profit. I gave all of the money, every penny, even above that which I had stolen, to my former employer. My boss said that while I had been in prison, he realized how sincerely sorry I was. He decided he would hire me back. I thanked him, but said that my family and I were returning to southern California. We needed a fresh start in a familiar place.

Making the transition back to normal life was even harder than I expected. Few people were willing to hire a convicted felon. To my surprise, Billy's company hired me as an accountant. Billy vouched for my integrity, putting his reputation on the line.

My family moved into a modest home in Billy's ward and the first thing we hung on the wall of our living room was the painting of Billy's baptism day.

Billy and I spent hours together over the next few weeks in the bishop's office, praying together, talking about all the things we had learned about the Savior and the Atonement. As a kid, Billy saved me physically in the ocean. Years later, as a grown man, and a bishop, he helped save me spiritually, helping me return to full fellowship in the Church. It made me realize that, in the end, it's all about enduring to the end.

"Did you know that just one little word has helped keep the shampoo industry thriving?" he told me during one of our weekly visits.

"Really? What word is that?"

"Repeat. As in 'Lather. Rinse. Repeat.' The more people repeat, the more shampoo they buy. It's a little trick that's famous in the ad business. I've learned that in life, we need to 'Exercise Faith. Repent. Read Scriptures. Pray. Repeat.' We need to do it every day. You know who taught me that?"

"Who?"

"You did." Then he paused. "Kevin, the Lord has forgiven you. You know that, right?"

I did, I just couldn't speak. I felt the Spirit so strongly. All I could do was nod my head. Then he called me to be the ward financial clerk.

"Does this mean I can baptize my son in a few months?" I asked.

"Absolutely," he said. "In fact, your son and my son are getting baptized on the same day. We're going to follow tradition and do it in the ocean."

I walked out of his office feeling the same way I did when I received the priesthood years earlier. And on a brisk November day, Billy and I went to the beach and baptized our children.

This may be the story of Billy Blankenship's conversion, but when all's said and done, it's about my own conversion. No matter if we grow up in the Church or not, we are all converts. At some point, whether it's at age 8 or 12 or 22 or 38 or 88, we must become converted on our own. Choosing to follow the Lord is not an event, not a moment in time, but a daily—an hour-by-hour, minute-by-minute, second-by-second—process.

My downfall began by neglecting to do the little things that I knew I needed to do daily and weekly. You know, the simple stuff I was taught way back in Primary. My precipitous descent started so gradually, so imperceptibly—at least to me—just like that time when I nearly drowned in the ocean as a six-year-old kid. On the surface things seemed calm, but I never saw the insidious undertow awaiting me.

Every time I look at the painting of Billy's baptism, which is at least once a day, it reminds me of the covenant I made when I was eight years old and the responsibilities I took upon myself when I was 12 and received the priesthood. I think of the many people who have helped me: Brother and Sister Woodson, my parents, Danny, and, of course, Billy Blankenship—um, Bishop William J. Blankenship.

Every time I see Bishop Blankenship conducting sacrament meeting, I see a walking, talking miracle in a navy blue suit and striped tie. If Billy blankety-blank Blankenship could wind up as a bishop, believe me, anything in this life is possible. If only the people in our childhood ward—especially the string of exasperated Primary teachers—could see him now.

Sister Browning had predicted that he would one day be a great leader. She was right. What makes him great is that he's always looking out for other Billy Blankenships out there—troubled people who need to be taught correct principles, people, like me, like all of us, who need unconditional love and support.

After one of my visits with Bishop Blankenship, I looked up the parable Sister Browning had taught me so many years ago, from the Book of Luke.

"What man of you, having an hundred sheep, if he lose one of them, doth not leave the ninety and nine in the wilderness, and go after that which is lost, until he find it?

"And when he hath found it, he layeth it on his shoulders, rejoicing.

"And when he cometh home, he calleth together his friends and neighbours, saying unto them, Rejoice with me; for I have found my sheep which was lost.

"I say unto you, that likewise joy shall be in heaven over one sinner that repenteth, more than over ninety and nine just persons, which need no repentance."

My perspective on the lost sheep had changed dramatically since the first time I heard that parable.

Over the course of three decades, Billy taught me about the power of Jesus Christ's love and His Atonement. He taught me that we are all children of God, no matter how we look or what we do. Billy helped me see the vast potential that lies dormant in all of us. Now, driving a fancy car and owning a mansion don't matter to me.

Jesus said, "In my Father's house are many mansions." That's good enough for me. My greatest desire is to stand before the Lord with confidence, with clean hands and a pure heart.

While I was incarcerated, I began writing a lot in my journal—the same one Sister Browning had given me years ago—about my experiences with the gospel. I wrote about an experience from my childhood. I titled it "The Lost Sheep."

If you haven't figured it out already, The Lost Sheep referred to in the title of this book isn't Billy Blankenship.

It's me.

In essence, aren't we all lost sheep? Doesn't the Savior, through the Atonement, constantly leave the ninety and nine and find us, individually? Whether our sins are large or small, He never gives up on us.

I remember learning in Primary that Jesus Christ loves everyone, especially children. I learned about Jesus Christ taking upon Himself all of the sins of every person who ever lived, and who would ever live, in this world.

I realize now that *I* made Christ suffer. *I* made Him bleed at every pore. *I* put those nail prints in His hands and feet. You know what the most amazing thing is? That the Savior could love someone like me.

About The Author

Jeff Call is a *Deseret News* sports writer who lives in central Utah with his wife, CherRon, and their six sons.

He served an LDS mission to Chile and later graduated with a bachelor's degree in journalism from BYU.

His is also the author of the novels *Mormonville, Return to Mormonville,* and *Rolling with the Tide*.

Jeff welcomes comments at jeff_call_2000@yahoo.com.